Truth Buried in the Dust

How One Man Took Down Tammany

Donald I. Zebe

Truth Buried in the Dust: How One Man Took Down Tammany Corruption

Copyright © 2025 by Donald Zebe

All rights reserved. No part of this book may be reproduced, stored in a retrieval system, or transmitted in any form or by any means, electronic, mechanical, photocopying, recording, or otherwise, without the prior written permission of the publisher, except in the case of brief quotations used in critical articles, reviews, or scholarly work.

This is a work of historical fiction. While it is rooted in real events, people, and places, certain names, characters, incidents, dialogue, and timelines have been dramatized, combined, or altered for narrative purposes. Any resemblance to actual persons, living or dead, beyond the historical figures portrayed, is coincidental.

For information, permissions, or bulk orders, please contact:

LCCN 2025923758

ISBNs 9781807210052 (eBook)

9781807210069 (Paperback)

9781807210076 (Hardcover)

Published by Red Rock Publishers

DISCLAIMER

Truth Buried in the Dust is a work of historical fiction inspired by real events and real historical figures.

Many individuals, institutions, places, and incidents depicted in this novel are drawn from documented history, including newspaper accounts, public records, and archival sources from the nineteenth century. However, for narrative purposes, certain events have been condensed, timelines adjusted, and dialogue imagined. In some cases, composite characters have been created to represent broader historical forces or viewpoints.

Any interpretation of motive, intent, or private conduct is fictional unless otherwise supported by historical record. This novel does not claim to be a definitive historical account, nor does it assert factual conclusions beyond what the available documentation reasonably supports.

The purpose of this work is to explore the intersection of truth, power, and justice during a period when records themselves were instruments of control—and to consider how history is shaped not only by what is written, but by what is withheld.

DEDICATION

To the descendants of **David H. Crowley**, whose courage echoes across generations.

To **Lillian Teresa Crowley**, who carried her father's quiet strength forward a bridge between the hardships he endured and the family she helped build with **Alexander Victor Sylvius Zebe**.*

And to **George Bliss Crowley**, named for the man who once believed that the truth could bend but never break and who passed his own steadfast heart to **Mary Agnes Duggan**,* with whom he shaped a legacy of integrity, resilience, and unshakable family loyalty.

This book belongs to all who came after them the grandchildren, great-grandchildren, great-great-grandchildren and the many yet to come who still carry the name, the stories, and the relentless promise that justice, once pursued, is never truly lost.

Prologue
Truth Buried in The Dust

Bronx, New York- March, 1998

The attic smelled of mothballs, paper dust, and the kind of secrets that wait too long to be found.

The air was stale, still, like the breath of a courtroom just before the verdict. Light spilled through the grime-caked window in long, slanted beams, illuminating boxes sealed with tape older than most memories.

Lillian Teresa hadn't planned to stay long. Just one last pass-through before the house hit the market. The brick walk-up on East 142nd Street had belonged to her grandmother, Lillian Zebe Marco, known simply as Sis. She had passed two months earlier at age ninety-three. Still sharp. Still stubborn.

Lillian's mother, Jane, had lived here too, right up until her marriage to Walter Fisher. Three generations of stories. One small house. But it wasn't just about the boxes. Or the furniture. Or even the memories.

It was about the photo that had always hung over the fireplace.

A Union soldier. A US Secret Service agent. A US Marshal. A NYPD detective Sergeant. Medals on his chest. No stories on his lips.

His name, never spoken with ease, always part reverence, part rumor.

David H. Crowley.

She knew the name. Every branch of the family did.

It hung in the air like incense, smoke from a fire long since put out, but never forgotten.

The story, as it had been whispered, went something like this:

Tammany Hall. A scandal. A sentence. A retraction. A war hero turned ghost. Cleared, eventually. But too late. Always too late.

That was all they ever said. If they said anything at all.

But upstairs, buried behind a stack of Civil Defense rations and a broken lamp, she found a box that changed everything.

Wrapped in dried oilskin. Latched in tarnished brass. Heavy, not just with dust, but with purpose.

She opened it carefully, knees creaking against the floorboards.

Inside:

A small, dulled NYPD detective's badge.

A Colt Navy revolver, wrapped in linen, dangerous even in silence.

A sepia photograph of a woman holding two children, their eyes heavy with knowing.

A stack of red-covered ledgers, the pages yellowed and the corners curled.

And at the bottom, sealed in wax: "M. Morris , Unsubmitted."

She held her breath.

Everyone in the family knew that name.

Maggie Morris, the witness who had damned her great-great-grandfather in court. She cracked the seal, fingers trembling.

The letter was dated March 3, 1885.

The signature was Maggie's. But this wasn't a confession.

It was a retraction.

A reversal of everything.

The lie exposed. The story undone. The buried truth, gasping for light after more than a century.

She looked at the revolver. The badge. The ledgers.

This wasn't memorabilia. It was evidence.

She lifted the top ledger, red and cracked, and opened it to the first page. Her ancestor's handwriting stared back at her, firm, slanted, deliberate:

"Not finished. Not yet."

The Other Side of the Bloodline

The attic creaked again. A second pair of feet on the stairs.

Donald Zebe, her cousin, ducked under the wooden beam. Tall, lean, and tired from too many years in archives and court records. He carried the other side of the family legacy, the line from Alexander V.S. Zebe, who had married Lillian Teresa Crowley, daughter of the Sergeant himself.

While Lillian Teresa carried Sis's name, Donald carried the war, a lifetime spent tracking the story through cemeteries, family Bibles, microfilm, and sealed court records.

"You found it?" he asked, his voice low.

She nodded, then handed him the retraction. He read it once. Then again. Silent.

"This changes everything."

She nodded again.

"He never stopped building his case. Even after they buried him."

They stood together, cousins from opposite branches of the same bloodline. One bore the name. The other bore the work. And now, they carried the story together.

What the courts didn't finish, they would.

What history forgot, they would remember.

David H. Crowley

Corporal, 69th NY Infantry , NYPD Detective

Falsely Accused. Honorably Remembered.

The city buried his name.

His family didn't.

And now, neither would history.

Chapter 1
Baptism at Gettysburg

July 2, 1863 Gettysburg, Pennsylvania

The sun had not yet burned through the heavy Pennsylvania mist when David Crowley crouched behind a battered stone wall on Cemetery Ridge, the dew still clinging to his boots like the last remnants of childhood. Sixteen, though the army clerk had written down seventeen to keep the muster rolls clean. No one asked questions when the Irish showed up to fight, especially not from the slums of Manhattan's East Side.

He was a boy dressed in a man's war, and the uniform didn't fit. The wool sagged at the shoulders, hung loose at the chest, and pinched at the thighs when he ran. But it was Union blue, and it came with a rifle and a name stitched in reputation, the Fighting 69th, a unit born from hunger and hard labor, from Catholic prayers whispered behind locked doors and curses hurled at English landlords. He wore that name like armor.

By dawn, he could taste the smoke. By midmorning, he could taste blood.

The first shell had landed somewhere to the left, near the peach orchard, announcing the Confederate arrival with a thunderclap that shook the ground. The second whistled overhead and exploded behind them, a spray of earth and bone scattering into the sky.

Sergeant O'Connor, a grizzled Irishman from County Clare with fists like fence posts and a voice like gravel, was murmuring a prayer in Gaelic. David couldn't make out the words, but the rhythm calmed him. Something about saints, maybe. Or death.

"You ever been in a real fight, Crowley?" the sergeant asked, not taking his eyes off the smoke-shrouded tree line.

Crowley's fingers tightened around his musket. His throat was dry, his stomach empty since the night before.

"No," he said. "Not like this."

O'Connor nodded. "Then today's your baptism."

Crowley didn't reply. The words hung in the air like prophecy.

The 69th had been moved forward too soon. Everyone knew it, even if no one would say it aloud. General Daniel Sickles, hero of Antietam, scandal of Washington, one-legged legend of too many saloons, had ordered the maneuver without clearance. Military men would later call it reckless, tactically unsound, a violation of the chain of command. But Sickles hadn't cared then, and he wouldn't care later. He moved when he thought the moment demanded it. And now the Irish boys of the 69th found themselves in the wrong place at the worst time.

The Confederate line began to materialize from the forest like a waking nightmare. They didn't come in a rush. That would've made it easier. Instead, they advanced with grim patience, step by step, bayonets glinting silver under the haze. Rebel yells rose like wolves in the hills.

Crowley raised his musket and fired into the smoke, not knowing whether he hit flesh or tree. A man beside him, a boy, really, maybe a few months older, was shot through the mouth and collapsed wordlessly. Another caught a fragment of cannon shell in the thigh and howled for a mother who would never know where he'd died.

It didn't feel like glory. It didn't feel like history. It felt like chaos.

Crowley fired again and again until the musket kicked so hard his shoulder throbbed. Then, when there was no time to reload, he thrust his bayonet forward and ran.

They met the Rebels just past the ridge, in a frenzy of smoke and steel. Crowley plunged the blade into a man's chest, too fast to see the color of his eyes. The body folded, and for a moment, the musket was stuck, tethering him to the man he'd just killed.

Another Rebel came screaming at him. Crowley wrenched the weapon free and swung like he was splitting firewood, catching the man in the jaw. Teeth and blood sprayed the air. The man went down twitching.

And just like that, it was survival. No sides. No flags. No drums. Just the savage arithmetic of kill or be killed.

Later, he wouldn't remember how long it lasted. Minutes, maybe. Hours. He was struck across the ribs with a rifle butt, crawled through a ditch of blood and splinters, saw Sergeant O'Connor fall and rise again like a man too stubborn for death. All the while, Sickles shouted behind them, barking orders between puffs of his cigar, dragging his mangled leg like an afterthought. The general had been shot years before, and the surgeons had taken the leg at the hip. He'd kept the bone, preserved in formaldehyde, and brought it with him wherever he went, a grotesque mascot for a man who had stared death down and won.

Then came the cannon blast that changed everything. Crowley never saw it. Just a sudden flash of white, a roar in his skull, and the taste of iron in his mouth. He woke with his face buried in the mud, ears ringing, hands trembling around a shattered musket. All around him, the world had quieted, like the battle had passed him by.

But the line had held. Somehow, against the weight of numbers and the weight of fear, the 69th had not broken.

At dusk, the clouds parted and a shaft of sunlight touched the ridge like a benediction. Sickles came limping up the hill, dragging what remained of his leg, still smoking the same cigar. He surveyed the ruins, the torn earth, the broken bodies, the boys who had become men in the space of an afternoon.

His eyes found Crowley, slumped against the stone wall, bloodied, filthy, his left eye swelling shut.

There was a flicker of recognition.

"I know you," Sickles said slowly. "You're that courthouse kid. The climber."

Crowley blinked, mud caked across his face.

Sickles grinned. "New York. 1861. Jay Gould. You went through the transom, handed him the writ. Hell of a move."

Crowley nodded weakly.

Sickles chuckled, then knelt beside him. "Told you to come find me if you ever needed a favor. Didn't think it'd be here."

Crowley tried to speak, but his throat was too dry. Sickles clapped him on the shoulder and rose.

"You've got guts, lad," he said. "Damn rare thing these days."

It wasn't a medal. It wasn't a commendation. But it meant something. A general's hand on his shoulder. A recognition that this day, this baptism, would mark him.

Not just as a soldier. But as someone who had survived the impossible.

Chapter 2
Aftermath

July 4, 1863 Camp Behind Cemetery Ridge, Pennsylvania

The war had paused, but the land hadn't noticed. Rain fell in sheets, drumming against the canvas of David Crowley's makeshift tent like distant artillery. The ground beneath him was soft with mud and blood and something else he didn't care to name.

Inside, the air stank of sweat, smoke, and the rot of unwashed bodies. The surgeons were still working in the tent across the path. Every so often, someone screamed. Every so often, they didn't. Either way, the blade kept moving.

Crowley sat alone near the edge of camp, his legs crossed under him, one hand nursing a tin cup of diluted whiskey, the other still caked in a dried crust of someone else's blood. He hadn't bothered to wash. There were no clean uniforms left, and besides, it seemed dishonest. Like pretending it hadn't happened.

The Fourth of July.

Back home, boys from his neighborhood were probably setting off firecrackers, hanging bunting from porches, tossing cheap flags into the air like the whole country hadn't just bled out on the hills of Pennsylvania.

But in Gettysburg, the celebration sounded different. Louder. Angrier. He knew the sound of celebration, and this wasn't it. The Confederates, stubborn to the end, had opened up again during the night, maybe out of spite, maybe because they didn't know what else to do. The guns had finally gone quiet around dawn, replaced by the low, grunting rhythm of burial. No ceremony. No final words. Just shallow graves and silence.

Crowley didn't sleep.

His body wanted it, his muscles throbbed, his feet ached, but his mind wouldn't release its grip. Every time he closed his eyes, he saw a face. Not one he knew. Just a face. Pale. Mouth open. Eyes wide in that awful, unblinking stare. A Confederate. Maybe eighteen. Maybe thirty. Crowley couldn't be sure. The bayonet hadn't asked.

They'd held the ridge. That's what the officers said. That was the word passed down through ranks like a blessing, we *held the ridge*. But no one felt like they'd won. Not the men still bleeding in the tents. Not the men digging the graves. Not the few who were whole enough to sit upright by the fire and drink what was left of the rations.

Across from him, a pair of boots appeared, polished, out of place, arrogant in their cleanliness. Crowley looked up slowly, his eyes catching the dark blue coat, the ivory-handled cane, the curled lips of a man used to smiling in the face of ruin.

General Daniel Sickles.

The man's legend moved faster than his limp. Hero. Scoundrel. Murderer. Congressman. They said he'd shot his wife's lover in Lafayette Park and still made it to dinner on time. That he'd used the trial to invent the insanity defense, walked free, and shook hands with Lincoln before the week was out. A man like that wasn't supposed to survive a battlefield. But there he was, grinning through cigar smoke like the devil's lawyer.

"We meet again."

Crowley nodded once.

"You shot the runner near Devil's Den," Sickles continued. "Sharp eye. Saved lives."

Crowley didn't answer. Praise felt like a trick, a lever waiting to be pulled.

Sickles took a seat without asking. The fire cracked between them, soft light dancing along the trim of his jacket. He tapped ash into the mud.

"You ever think about life after this?" the general asked.

Crowley looked into the flames. The whiskey sloshed gently in his cup. "No, sir."

"You should." Sickles leaned in, voice lowering like a man about to offer a bribe. "This war ends eventually. Not soon, not clean. But it ends. And when it does, you're not going back to bakeries and butcher shops. Not men like you."

Crowley didn't speak.

"There are other wars," Sickles said. "Quieter ones. Wars fought in alleys and back rooms, behind desks and courthouse doors. And they need men who don't flinch."

From inside his coat, Sickles produced a folded paper. No seal. No regiment. Just a name scrawled across the bottom in dark ink:

E. M. Stanton. Secretary of War.

"Report when you're ready," he said, handing it over. "Ask for the back office. You'll find work. The kind no one talks about."

Crowley took it. Didn't open it. Just slid it into the inside pocket of his coat like it was any other scrap of paper. He didn't ask questions. Sickles liked that.

By the time the general limped away, the whiskey was gone. The fire had died down to embers. The rain was steady now, honest in its rhythm.

The boy who had stormed Cemetery Ridge was gone. Buried, maybe, with the others. What remained was something different, quieter, colder. Something built not just to survive, but to serve.

Before dawn, Crowley wrote a letter home. He never signed it. Never sent it. Just folded it and left it tucked under a rock beside the graves.

Then he walked away.

No ceremony. No salute. Just one last look at the tent flaps billowing in the wind and a bitter truth under his breath.

"War doesn't end," he muttered. "It just changes shape."

And with that, David Crowley disappeared into the morning mist, just another survivor carrying more than he could name.

Chapter 3
The General's Favor

August 1865, New York City

The war had ended, but the peace was unfinished.

Every train that pulled into the city carried pieces of it, shattered men with thousand-yard stares, coats that no longer fit, boots worn thin from marching. Some carried medals. Most carried ghosts. David Crowley stepped off the troop train at Castle Garden with nothing but a half-healed scar on his shoulder and a duffel bag that smelled of powder and rain.

The city welcomed them back with indifference.

Manhattan was not a place to pause. It pulsed, restless, grimy, alive. The wharves overflowed with cargo and men; street peddlers shouted in six languages; political ward bosses greased palms and swapped names like playing cards. Five Points stank of whiskey and blood. The Bowery boiled over with gamblers, pickpockets, and immigrants packed ten to a room. For most, the war had been distant thunder, noise on the horizon while they fought a different battle: survival.

Crowley had changed, though. Not in ways the world could see. His bones felt older. His eyes no longer darted like a boy's. He didn't flinch at the sharp crack of a dropped barrel or the scream of a drunk stumbling into an alley fight. Something inside him had calcified, something you didn't get back, no matter how many medals they hung around your neck.

Two weeks after his return, the summons came.

It wasn't written on letterhead or wrapped in ribbon. Just a folded note, delivered by a boy with sharp eyes and sharper elbows, no older than ten, who vanished into the crowd as fast as he'd appeared.

General Sickles requests your presence. One o'clock. No excuses.

Crowley stared at the words for a long time. No address. Just a corner, Broadway and Warren. That was enough. It always was.

He considered ignoring it.

But you didn't ignore Daniel Sickles.

The borrowed law office sat on the second floor above a pawnbroker's and a brothel that had stopped pretending to be anything else. The stairs creaked with each step, steep and narrow and lined with shadows. The door was cracked open.

Inside, the room smelled of old tobacco and damp paper. Law books lined the walls, hundreds of them, but not a single one had dust disturbed on its spine. Sickles wasn't the type to reference precedent.

He sat behind a massive oak desk, one booted leg up, the other, the wooden one, propped awkwardly to the side. Smoke drifted from a half-burnt cigar clamped between his teeth. His coat was open, his waistcoat stained with last night's whiskey. His eyes, though, were razor-sharp.

"Well," he drawled, "look what the war dragged in."

Crowley stood in the doorway, uncertain. He hadn't seen Sickles since Gettysburg. The general hadn't changed, except now he looked less like a field commander and more like what he truly was: a man who survived anything, even his own reputation.

Sickles waved him in with a flick of the wrist.

"Not even old enough to drink legally, and already you've stared down the devil."

Crowley didn't answer. He stepped forward, stiff and cautious. The general took another puff and studied him through the haze.

"You've grown," Sickles said. "The shoulders tell it. And the eyes, those have aged ten years."

"I don't feel different," Crowley lied.

Sickles smiled. "That's the trick of it, son. The body forgets. The soul keeps score."

He leaned forward, resting both elbows on the desk. The banter faded. The room grew quiet.

"You ever think about what comes next?" Sickles asked.

Crowley frowned. "Next?"

"The musket's behind you. The marching's done. No more drumbeats. No more bugles. You're a free man."

"I'm not sure I know what that means."

"Exactly," Sickles said, tapping ash into a chipped tumbler. "That's why I asked you here."

He opened a drawer and retrieved a small wooden box. Inside was a single card, off-white, thick, crisp. He set it on the table and turned it slowly so Crowley could read the words.

United States Secret Service.

No seal. No flourish. Just the title, and beneath it, a name scrawled in careful ink: Stanton.

"The battlefield's not the only place where the Union bleeds," Sickles said. "There's rot in Washington. Counterfeiters printing currency by the wagonload. Spies who never surrendered. Political men willing to sell their country for a sliver of power."

He paused, letting the words sink in.

"There's a quiet war, Crowley. One we'll never win with sabers. We need men who can follow orders, keep their mouths shut, and do what needs doing."

Crowley's fingers hovered over the card. He didn't touch it yet.

"What makes you think I'm that man?"

"Because you didn't die at Gettysburg," Sickles said flatly. "You didn't run. You didn't break. You held. I've seen a hundred officers with college degrees crumble at less."

He rose slowly, his wooden leg groaning as he shifted weight. Limping around the desk, he stopped in front of Crowley, lowering his voice.

"I don't need saints. I need survivors. Men who know what it means to look death in the eye and walk away."

He held up the card again.

"This isn't a commission. No uniform, no parade. If you say yes, you disappear from the rolls. You answer to Stanton. And only Stanton. You see things you can't unsee. You do things no one will ever thank you for."

"And if I say no?" Crowley asked.

"Then you walk out that door," Sickles said. "And try to make peace with the world. But between you and me, I don't think the world's ever going to be peaceful for someone like you."

Crowley said nothing.

Sickles gave him the card anyway.

That night, Crowley sat on a cot in a narrow room at the edge of Five Points, the kind of boarding house where the floors slanted and the wallpaper peeled like dead skin. The river was visible through a cracked window, moonlight bouncing off the oily current.

The card lay on the table beside a pocketknife and a folded letter he'd started a dozen times and never finished. The lamp cast a weak glow, flickering against the water-stained walls.

No orders.

No glory.

Just a name.

A trust.

A doorway.

And he knew, with a slow, settling certainty, that he would walk through it.

He tucked the card into the inside pocket of his coat.

He didn't sleep.

He was eighteen.

Too young to understand the weight of silence.

Too hardened to fear it.

And as he stared out at the river, the city churning beneath him, Crowley understood what Sickles meant. The war had changed shape. And now, so had he.

Chapter 4
Into the Fog

The office of the United States Secret Service wasn't what Crowley expected. No brass nameplates. No marble floors. Just two cramped rooms above a hardware store on Broome Street, smelling of damp coal and betrayal. The wallpaper curled like old scabs, yellowed with age. A single window looked out onto an alley where rats outnumbered honest men.

Chief Inspector William P. Wood sat behind a battered desk piled high with files, smudged ink, and half-eaten sandwiches. He was a man carved from old timber, rough, unyielding, and full of splinters. Wood didn't waste words.

"You sure you're up for this?"

Crowley didn't flinch. "If I wasn't, I wouldn't be sitting here."

Wood grunted and slid a folder across the desk. "Then read fast. We're already behind."

Across the top: FENIANS.

The Fenian Brotherhood had risen like smoke from the battlefields of the Civil War. Born of the Irish Republican Brotherhood in Ireland, its American counterpart was a seething coalition of disillusioned Union veterans, Catholic hardliners, and exiles carrying the weight of ancestral vengeance. Many had fought under the flags of Meagher's Irish Brigade, the Corcoran Legion, and the 69th New York. Now, they turned their discipline toward a new target: Canada.

Two names loomed large in their ranks.

John Francis O'Mahony, scholar turned soldier, had once fought in the Young Irelander Rebellion of 1848 before serving in the American Civil War. He gave everything to the Irish cause, his fortune, his peace, even his reputation. Revered as the mind of the movement, he lived in near-poverty, but his word carried weight.

Thomas J. Kelly was different, sharper, hungrier. A soldier by instinct, he joined the IRB at war's end and quickly rose to Colonel. The Brotherhood sent him to Ireland to test its readiness; his brutal assessments earned him authority, and when he returned to the States, he carried himself like a revolutionary general.

These men gave the Brotherhood not just legitimacy, but danger.

The plan was audacious: invade British Canada with thousands of Irish-American veterans, seize territory, and ransom it for Irish independence. They had stockpiled arms, built a war chest fed by sympathizers in New York, Boston, and Chicago. Between 1860 and 1867, they raised more than half a million dollars, enough to buy weapons, ships, and political silence.

If they succeeded, it would ignite war with Britain, and drag the United States into the fire. Lincoln was gone. Reconstruction was fragile. The Union could not survive another war.

Wood tapped the folder. "We need a ghost. Someone who can drink like a Fenian, curse like one, bleed like one, and vanish when it's done."

Crowley nodded. "When do I start?"

His cover was brutal, but believable: a battle-worn Irish corporal. Bitter. Abandoned. Still angry at the promises the Union never kept. He stopped shaving. Let his brogue return, thick and ragged. He picked fights in dockside saloons, won a few, lost one, bled enough to earn his place.

Chapter 5
The Masquerade

December 1867 – New York, Buffalo, Troy

By December, Crowley was no longer just playing a part. He was buried in it.

He spoke in clipped Irish slang, rolled his Rs like a Belfast dockworker, and sang rebel songs with a grit that made even the old fighters nod in reverence. Every morning, he rehearsed his cover story as if reciting scripture, his village, his "lost" brother in Kilmainham, his hatred for the Crown. Lies laced with just enough truth to make them bleed.

The Fenian world was layered like sediment, quiet on the surface, combustible beneath. His days were spent posing as a courier, a carpenter, a cousin of someone no one could place but everyone swore they remembered. At night, he knelt in candlelit crypts and bowed his head not in prayer, but in strategy. Whispered plans passed like contraband: Montreal by Christmas. Quebec by fire. Always coded. Always sacred.

Secrecy wasn't just survival. It was currency.

He learned to read a man's allegiance by how he folded his hands or passed a pint. A twitch at the wrong word, a blink too long, these were tells. So Crowley made himself unreadable. He drank what they drank. He sang what they sang. He even took a beating once outside an Albany pub after refusing to curse Queen Victoria with enough venom. The blood bought him trust.

Buffalo was colder than it had any right to be. The wind came off the lake like a British saber, slicing through coats and conversation. But beneath St. Dominic's Church, where the crypt had been hollowed out into an armory, the air was stifling. Crowley crouched beside crates stamped *Chapel Wine* that were packed tight with .58 caliber Enfields. He catalogued them in silence, one by one, by candlelight, while behind him, men prayed in Irish and sharpened bayonets on worn whetstones.

In Albany, he found the uniforms, dozens of them. Red-coated, brass-buttoned frauds stitched in sweatshops and meant to sew confusion into Canadian lines. He lifted the manifest from a quartermaster too fond of gin and stashed it in a hollowed-out hymnal. Every move he made, he pictured a hangman's knot waiting on the other end.

Troy was worse.

There, in the belly of a tavern named *The Apostle's Cask*, Crowley watched two men, Cathal Burke and Sean Greeley, fill beer barrels with blasting powder and nails. They joked in Gaelic as they worked, not knowing Crowley had already wired a signal to the Secret Service, scrawled in lemon juice across the label of a wine bottle. All it needed was heat to reveal.

But every message he sent, every report he filed, was a risk. And the wolves were always sniffing.

One night in Schenectady, the shadows turned on him. Two scouts, barely men, but with eyes hard as iron, dragged him into an alley behind a cobbler's shop. The knife they used to tear open his coat was the same kind he'd seen buried in Loyalist spines.

"What's your mother's name?" one asked.

He hesitated just long enough.

"Margaret," he said, then added, "from Bantry. Died in childbirth. My sister raised me, poor soul."

It was the truth. Just not his.

They let him go, but he didn't sleep for days. That same week, a letter meant for a trusted contact, its code embedded in the margins of a psalm, was intercepted by a priest who wasn't supposed to read it. Crowley burned his coat in an alley behind St. Mark's and went to ground on the docks, hiding in the hold of a Dutch freighter under sacks of rotting oranges.

The worst part wasn't the fear.

It was the belonging.

They called him brother. They raised toasts in his name. O'Mahony himself had clapped him on the shoulder in a cellar on the Bowery and called him "a lion of the 69th." That night, Crowley had laughed, clinked his glass, and felt something crack inside his ribs.

Because deep down, some of it wasn't a lie.

He had bled for Ireland. He had killed for it. He had lost men on the fields of Virginia who whispered Gaelic as they died. And now he walked among their kin, feeding them just enough false hope to derail the dream they'd built their lives on.

Each step forward was betrayal. Each delay he sowed, each map he stole, each shipment he rerouted, these were the nails in the coffin of their revolution. But it had to be done. If they marched on Canada, there would be blood. Thousands would die. And worse, it would fracture Irish solidarity across the diaspora.

So Crowley pressed deeper into the masquerade. Each night, he became the role. He played the patriot. He sharpened his false accent like a weapon.

And he prayed, not for salvation, but that when this was over, the ghosts he was making would stay quiet.

Chapter 6
The Judas Question

Late December, 1867 – Buffalo

It started with a glance. Just a glance, too long, too sharp. But in a world of whispers and assassins, a glance could be lethal.

Crowley was hunched over a crate of rifles in the undercroft of St. Dominic's when he noticed it. Michael O'Laughlin, one-eyed, half-drunk, and twice as dangerous, stood across the room, pretending to polish his revolver. But his gaze was locked. Not on the weapons. On him.

Crowley didn't flinch.

He wrapped the last of the Enfields in burlap and lit a cigarette with fingers that didn't dare tremble. He offered one to O'Laughlin, but the man waved it off, muttering something about smoke drawing British scouts.

That was the first sign.

The second came three nights later, after a planning session disguised as a rosary vigil. Bridget Cahill passed him a missive, standard drop, standard code, but her eyes didn't match the warmth in her voice. They flicked to the door. Measuring distance.

Inside the note was a line that hadn't appeared before:

"What burns cannot lie."

It was a code test. The kind used when a mole was suspected.

Crowley didn't sleep. He didn't eat. He spent two days wandering Buffalo's Irish quarter, searching for neutral ground, safer shadows. But nowhere felt safe anymore. Not even the rooftop of the bakery where he'd once passed a hundred rounds through a flour sack while boys below sold bread.

That night, he returned to the rectory basement beneath the chapel, where strategy was inked in invisible scripts on hymnals and maps were drawn in dust on cellar floors. There were fewer men than usual. No one said it, but something had shifted. The silence had weight.

Then O'Laughlin stood.

"One of us is ash in the bread," he said. No names. No accusations. Just the kind of phrase that makes a room go cold.

Crowley kept his eyes forward, jaw tight.

But the others looked. One by one, they glanced his way, Bridget last. Her hand hovered near the folds of her shawl, where Crowley knew she kept a single-shot Derringer dipped in lampblack.

O'Laughlin pulled out a scrap of parchment. On it, heat-revealed, was the mark of a failed message. One Crowley had thought had burned.

The priest in Albany had betrayed him. Not for loyalty to the Crown, but over a woman. A jealous confession. A turned coat. The letter intercepted, half-burned, and now damning.

Crowley stepped forward slowly.

"If you believe it's me," he said, "ask me what I said at Sharpsburg, when my captain bled out in the wheat field. Ask me how many of ours died at Fredericksburg in the muck. Ask me what I whispered to Father McGinty as he gave last rites to Tommy Doyle while he bled through his boots."

O'Laughlin squinted.

"You could've read those names in a dispatch."

"I buried those names."

Silence.

Then, a voice from the shadows, Father Flynn, the false priest with hands rougher than a blacksmith's. "Let him prove it."

"How?" Bridget asked.

Flynn pulled a lantern closer and held up a wax-sealed packet. "This came from Troy. It was meant for Montreal command. But it never arrived. Crowley was the courier."

Crowley's heart caught.

He had rerouted the packet, replacing the real contents with a forged blueprint for a border armory that didn't exist. The trap had been laid. But if they opened the seal and checked the contents, they'd find only lies.

And if they found the lies?

They'd bury him beneath the altar he prayed under.

Crowley stepped forward. "Open it."

Bridget blinked. "You want it opened?"

"I need it opened."

It was the only card left to play, reverse suspicion by leaning into the fire.

Flynn cracked the seal. Slowly. Pulled the parchment from within.

He read. His brow furrowed. He read again. Then looked up.

"God's teeth," he muttered. "This... this says the Canadians have fortified Richelieu Fort with Gatlings."

A ripple went through the room.

"That can't be true," O'Laughlin said.

"It's not," Crowley lied smoothly. "It's worse. They've tripled the garrison and moved naval reserves to the Saint Lawrence. I saw the rail manifests myself."

Bridget's grip on the Derringer loosened.

The moment passed.

Just barely.

But O'Laughlin still stared at him, that one eye burning like a coal in the dark.

After the meeting broke, Crowley made his way outside. Snow fell thick and slow. He walked three blocks before ducking into an alley and gripping the brick wall like it might hold him together.

He was alive.

For now.

But now they were watching. Every step. Every word. Every glance.

And from here on out, there would be no room for error.

The mask had to become the man.

Chapter 7
Ridgeway

June 1, 1867, Fort Erie, Ontario, Canadian Border

It was almost beautiful.

The sun broke across the Niagara like fire on glass. Men lined the docks with muskets on their backs and songs in their throats, ready to fight not for country, but for an idea. Ireland. Free and whole. Many had never set foot on its soil.

They still bled for it.

Crowley stood among them, uniformed like the rest in faded Union blues, a battered campaign hat low over his brow. The air smelled of gun oil and pine pitch. The assault was no longer rumor. No longer theory.

The invasion was real.

Rifles had come up the Erie Canal under cover of darkness. Powder kegs hidden in barrels of molasses. The Fenians had crossed the Niagara the night before, some in rowboats, others on barges stolen from canal runners. By dawn on June 2nd, they had massed near the village of Ridgeway.

Crowley had less than twenty-four hours.

O'Laughlin was already across the river with nearly eight hundred men. Bridget Cahill had led the second wave north, a satchel of blueprints and coded field plans tied beneath her skirts. She'd kissed Crowley's cheek the night before, just once, and said, "We'll drink from the Saint Lawrence when this is over."

He'd smiled.

Then swallowed the bile rising in his throat.

Because it would never be over. Not if they crossed the line. Not if blood hit Canadian soil. The war they wanted would consume them. And the British would not respond with handcuffs. They would answer with fire.

So Crowley moved.

First, the comms.

He slipped away at twilight, riding west under the pretense of scouting railway lines. In truth, he was heading to a safehouse near Niagara Falls, a decommissioned postal relay run by a former Pinkerton. Inside was a cipher desk and a telegraph line buried beneath the floorboards, still live, still wired to the War Department.

It would be his last transmission.

TO: Treasury Dept. – NYS Field Contact – URGENT

SUBJECT: Fenian Invasion Active

Armed incursion at Fort Erie. Estimated 1,200 combatants.

Objective appears Ridgeway rail junction; northward pressure on Hamilton.

Immediate reinforcements advised: Canadian militia understrength.

Request border seal from Lewiston to Buffalo.

Signal detain Bridget Cahill (alias Mary Dunne) and M. O'Laughlin (alias Black Jack) if recovered.

May not survive.

, D.H.C.

He tore the page from the pad, sealed it in a copper tube, and fed it into the line.

The reply came ten minutes later. One word: **RECEIVED.**

He barely made it back to the ridge.

That night, smoke curled from makeshift campfires along a scrub line near Ridgeway. Some of the younger Fenians toasted the ghost of Wolfe Tone. Others prayed with calloused fingers wrapped around rosaries and rifle straps. Crowley sat in silence, across from a boy no older than seventeen who spoke only Irish and clutched a dagger forged from melted shoe nails.

Then came the order.

Form ranks at 0500.

Crowley stood with them.

The plan was simple: hit the Canadian rail line fast, push toward Hamilton, seize a telegraph station, and cut off response. They wore tattered Federal blues, many with insignia torn off, to confuse defenders.

But Crowley had done more than send a warning.

He had slipped false orders into Flynn's satchel, redirected units toward phantom crossings, and altered the rendezvous point for a key munitions wagon so it would arrive an hour too late.

It wasn't enough to warn. He had to fracture them.

And he did.

When the Fenians crested the ridge on June 2nd, they expected to meet scattered militia. Instead, they faced Canadian forces already in position, outnumbered but braced, bayonets fixed. The 13th Battalion waited in silence, boots planted in trampled hayfields still wet with morning dew.

The first shots cracked like cannon fire.

The skirmish that followed was brief. Bloody. Confused.

Crowley fought like a man possessed, because he had to. To break cover now would be suicide. So he fired over heads, jammed rounds, called phantom flanks. He shouted for medics who didn't exist. Smoke swallowed the field.

And by midmorning, it was over.

The Fenians broke. Splintered. Fled back toward Fort Erie in chaos.

Crowley went with them, blood on his coat and fire in his lungs. The wounded screamed from hay carts, and Bridget, her hair matted with blood, not her own, grabbed his arm and spat, "Somebody warned them. There's a rat."

His silence was answer enough.

That night, he vanished, slipping through marshes before the arrests began.

Three days later, Crowley stood on a freight dock in Buffalo, dressed as a longshoreman, coat turned, hat low.

He watched as Canadian authorities extradited Bridget Cahill under armed guard. He saw O'Laughlin limping, cuffed, still screaming about traitors.

And then he walked.

West. Away from the river. Away from the cause. Away from the fire he had helped ignite, and then snuff out.

He had saved lives.

But the ghosts followed.

And they all spoke with Irish tongues.

Chapter 8
The Speculator's Web

Manhattan, July 1869

Chambers Street Courthouse

The courthouse reeked of lies ironed into linen. Beneath the marble dome and brass gaslights, men spoke in hushed tones but moved with the arrogance of immunity. It wasn't justice they came for. It was theater.

And Jay Gould was center stage.

He sat at the defendant's table with the stillness of a coiled watch, thin fingers laced neatly, a faint smile carved into his face like a permanent mask. He didn't look like a man on trial. He looked like a man inspecting the gears of his next investment.

Crowley stood half-hidden behind a fluted column near the vestibule. He wore a gray summer coat and a wide-brimmed hat that shadowed his eyes. No badge. No authority. Just a ghost in the gallery. He wasn't listed as a witness. Bliss had made sure of that.

They hadn't met in a courtroom. They met in a hallway that smelled of coal dust and damp rope, two winters earlier, after midnight on Whitehall Street, when a lighter bound for Canada had been quietly unloaded under Treasury eyes. Crowley, fresh off an ugly stint running with Fenian couriers, had handed over a notebook of names that shouldn't have been in the same sentence, dock bosses, aldermen, a pair of federal clerks with elastic morals.

Bliss showed up without an entourage, a plain topcoat and a prosecutor's stare, the kind that measured a man's weight in seconds. "You're the one who doesn't blink," he said, as if that were a résumé. He read the notebook once, closed it, and asked a question no policeman ever had: "What didn't you write down?"

Crowley told him about the missing ledger pages, the bribes paid in credit at a riverfront grocer, a code stitched into the margins of shipping bills. He expected doubt. He got instructions.

"Write nothing else," Bliss said. "From now on, you talk to me, and only me."

A week later, in General Sickles's smoky parlor on Fifth Avenue, Bliss watched Crowley break a cipher with a stub of pencil and a glass pane held up to the fire. Sickles loved the drama. Bliss loved the method. He had the rare prosecutor's gift of recognizing a man who could live in two rooms at once, the room with the criminals and the room with the evidence.

They struck a bargain that night that never saw ink. Bliss would open doors Crowley wasn't supposed to know existed, Treasury rooms with no names on them, marshal's offices where warrants were folded into newspaper sleeves, banks that would unfreeze an account if Bliss merely stood in the lobby. In return, Crowley would go where reputations couldn't, cellars, back pews, the pockets of the city where money talked with its hat pulled low.

They were not friends. They were an instrument and a hand. Bliss tuned; Crowley cut. By the time Erie turned from rumor to war, each could finish the other's sentence with a look.

"You won't be in the papers," Bliss had told him in a dark booth at Fraunces Tavern. "And you won't be in the record. This time, you're the knife no one sees coming."

The Erie War wasn't a gunfight. It was financial trench warfare. Gould had illegally printed a hundred thousand shares of Erie Railroad stock, sold them into a bubble of his own making, and then greased half the legislature in Albany to legalize the fraud after the fact. Vanderbilt had tried to fight back, lost a million dollars and nearly choked on his own pride.

Bliss didn't need a policeman. He needed a bloodhound.

So Crowley went underground.

He followed the ink.

Clerks living on ten dollars a week suddenly leased Fifth Avenue apartments. Lawyers in Gould's orbit took "health retreats" to Saratoga, always after major votes. Crowley memorized faces, followed mistresses, tapped telegrams. He trailed them from the Union Trust Building to the Tammany Club to private parlors where liquor flowed and names were traded like poker chips.

And always, he listened.

In a freight yard near Hell's Kitchen, he found a discarded stock manifest listing ten thousand shares under fictitious initials. A day later, he bought a janitor at Gould's brokerage a new coat in exchange for a trash bin of torn receipts, most worthless, except one slip tied to a senator's blind trust.

But the coup came in the form of a brown ledger, no larger than a prayer book, hidden in a crawlspace above the Union League Club's wine cellar. He found it thanks to a trembling accountant who drank too much and wanted out of the city alive. The book was filled with names, dates, and cash transactions, legal on the surface, damning between the lines.

Crowley took it straight to Bliss.

They hid it in a Treasury safehouse behind a false panel in a Brooklyn tailor's shop. Bliss ran his fingers across the spine like a priest with a relic.

"This is the rope," he said. "Now we find the neck."

That's when Crowley found Patrick Dorn.

A failed bookmaker and former broker's runner, Dorn had ferried envelopes from Wall Street to Albany during the vote to retro-legitimize Gould's fraud. They met in a backroom oyster bar off Delancey, where the air stank of brine and brandy. Dorn's eye twitched as he spoke.

"Fifty envelopes," Dorn said. "Each with a name. Each marked 'YES.' That's all it took."

"What was in them?"

"More than I ever made moving paper. Hell, one senator bought a horse with his, a *white* one."

Crowley leaned in. "Do you still have anything? Anything physical?"

"God, no," Dorn said, his voice cracking. "But the bill passed two days later. That's proof enough, ain't it?"

Two nights later, Dorn disappeared.

Some said he'd taken a steamer south. Others said his body turned up near Pelham Bay, no teeth, no wallet. Crowley never found out.

But he got the message.

Gould's reach wasn't limited to ledgers. He played the long game. Paid small to win big. Hired enforcers who looked like butlers and assassins who walked like notaries.

Crowley changed coats three times a day. Rerouted his walks. Ate nowhere twice. He shaved his beard. Slept with a derringer under his pillow. Once, he caught a man tailing him after a courthouse session and led him into an alley behind a butcher shop. The man ended up with a blade at his throat.

"You want something cut?" Crowley asked.

The man ran.

The trial itself became a mockery of law, motions, delays, technicalities. Gould's lawyers were silver-tongued conjurors. They didn't argue facts. They redefined them.

But the tide began to shift when a telegram was intercepted between Gould's personal secretary and a New York judge.

Deliver green bouquet immediately.

It sounded harmless, until Treasury deciphered it.

The "bouquet" was twenty thousand dollars in bearer bonds. Wrapped in roses. Delivered to the judge's summer estate in Tarrytown.

A week later, a junior banker came forward with slips linking fraudulent deposits directly to Gould. It was the break they needed.

Until he died.

His carriage exploded outside the Fulton Ferry terminal. The Times called it faulty coal gas.

Crowley knew better.

Still, he pressed on, delivering statements, tracing accounts, narrowing the flow of capital like water through a funnel. The final week, the jury looked ready. The courthouse buzzed with the whiff of justice.

And then the judge ruled the ledger inadmissible.

"Improper chain of custody," he said, never once looking at the jury.

Bliss broke a chair against the courthouse wall that night.

"They bought the judge," he spat. "Goddamn them, they bought the bloody judge."

In the end, Gould paid a $5,000 fine, pocket change. No prison. No record. No real stain.

He left court flanked by two lawyers and the faintest trace of a smirk.

Crowley stood at the base of the marble steps as Gould passed.

The financier paused. Nodded, just once. A gesture of respect. Or maybe conquest.

Crowley didn't return it.

He turned, walked into the summer heat, and didn't look back.

Because the war wasn't over.

It had just gone deeper. Underground.

Chapter 9
Blood in the Ledger

New York City, Early Autumn, 1870

The summer faded, but the heat didn't break.

It just sank underground.

Crowley sat in a fourth-floor office above a pawn shop on Canal Street, sleeves rolled, collar open, a new ledger spread before him, red leather, unmarked, dangerous. It contained names, dates, coded references to judges, aldermen, railroad directors, and state officials, all cross-referenced against one source:

Tammany Hall.

He hadn't started with them. But that's where every trail led. Always. When you followed the money long enough in Manhattan, it ended behind the velvet curtains at the Tammany Club, or in the coat pocket of a man who wore a white carnation and smiled too often.

Gould may have escaped trial, but he'd paid for it, with favors.

And those favors went through Boss Tweed.

The Erie trial had been a win on paper and a failure in the streets. Gould walked free, his empire intact. But in the process, Crowley had seen the truth: the judges weren't lazy or merely bought, they were installed. The legislature wasn't just corruptible, it was owned.

And at the top of that pyramid sat William Magear Tweed.

Part senator. Part thief. All shadow.

Bliss knew it too.

"Tweed's smarter than Gould," he told Crowley in a backroom of Cooper Union. "Gould uses people. Tweed builds them. He makes kings out of paupers, and takes their loyalty in blood."

"Then we cut the artery," Crowley said.

It wasn't vengeance anymore.

It was survival.

Because Crowley was being watched.

Three times that month he spotted the same man on separate corners, once at City Hall, once near the Cooper Market, and again outside Mary Agnes's church. Always reading a paper. Always watching.

Then came the letter.

No envelope. Just a folded scrap tucked inside his coat when he wasn't looking.

You're digging graves. Careful whose you fall into.

, The Ring

He still had work to finish.

The Erie Railroad had been the proving ground. What came next was systemic: Tweed's men inside the Department of Public Works, the Board of Education, even the city's courthouse construction, thirteen million dollars spent on a building that didn't yet have a roof.

Crowley compiled everything, bribes laundered through contractors, judges whose mortgages were paid off the books, aldermen who signed blank checks in exchange for "loyalty incentives."

He recorded it all.

Names like Richard Connolly, the city comptroller, who moved funds between shell accounts with religious regularity. Peter Sweeny, Tweed's legal whisperer, who buried corruption in case law. Carmine "the Architect" Corsi, who bid on city projects before they were even publicly posted.

Crowley even found an ally, or thought he did. Elias Root, a bookkeeper for the city treasurer, with ulcers, three daughters, and a secret stash of municipal payout receipts.

"I never cashed them," Root confessed. "Too much blood on the paper."

Then Root disappeared.

His apartment ransacked. Ledgers gone. His daughters taken to live with a "benefactor."

Crowley burned his notes that night and rewrote them from memory.

He knew what was coming.

The closer he got to Tweed, the louder the silence around him grew. Friendly barkeeps stopped meeting his eye. A patrolman who once owed him his life suddenly didn't know his name. A magistrate delayed a subpoena twice, then hinted Crowley might want to leave the city "for his health."

But he stayed.

Because inside Tammany's operation, something new was taking shape, a network far bigger than railroad stock or street-repair graft. It wasn't just theft anymore. It was control.

Land. Water rights. Elections. Everything that flowed through New York now flowed through The Ring.

Bliss gave it the name. Crowley gave it his attention.

And if his instincts were right, the machine was about to test its full power in the mayoral race of 1872.

He closed the red ledger and locked it in a tin box beneath the floorboards. Then he looked out the window at the glowing gaslights of Manhattan.

The city was still alive.

But the cancer was spreading.

And Crowley was running out of time.

Chapter 10
Exposure

Summer 1871, New York City

It began with a packet left on the editorial desk at *The New York Times*.

No return address. No fingerprints.

Just a stack of invoices, ledgers, and vouchers bound in twine and sealed with old wax.

Someone knew exactly what they were delivering.

Inside: proof.

Real, impossible-to-ignore proof.

Courthouse construction bills inflated beyond reason.

Stonework charged three times over.

Carpentry billed by men who didn't exist.

A city paying thirteen million dollars for a building that should've cost three, and every dollar funneled back into the pockets of one man and the machine that protected him.

William Magear Tweed.

Boss. Alderman. Senator. Thief.

And behind him, contracts bearing the faint initials of every friend he had in City Hall.

The editor went pale. They had published attacks before, cartoons, satire, cautious exposés, but this was different.

This wasn't rumor. It was a weapon.

It was too clean, too structured, too surgical.

It was *prepared*.

It was Crowley.

For weeks, Crowley had worked in secret.

He'd followed the trail from a bribe-slicked city clerk to a stone supplier whose bills didn't match the quarry output, to a dead contractor whose signature still authorized payments.

He'd lifted names off voter rolls and matched them to ghost employees in the Department of Public Works.

He met contacts in alleys, on rooftops, in shuttered taverns.

Every night, he added more to the dossier.

His handwriting was tight, disciplined, like confession, but colder.

And when it was done, he didn't take it to Bliss.

He didn't take it to a judge.

He took it to the one institution with just enough backbone left to swing at Tammany:

The New York Times.

No note. No name.

The documents would speak for themselves.

July 1871.

The headline struck like a thunderclap:

THE TWEED RING UNMASKED: $13 MILLION STOLEN FROM CITY COFFERS

By midmorning, the mayor's office was under siege.

By noon, Tweed was giving interviews, denying everything.

By nightfall, the city was boiling.

Crowley watched it unfold from a rooftop near City Hall. A storm was coming, not from the sky, but from the streets.

Shouts echoed off the stone.

"*Thief!*" "*Traitor!*" "*Blood money!*"

Men who once toasted Tweed were burning his posters in the gutters.

But Crowley didn't celebrate.

He knew better.

This wasn't victory.

It was provocation.

And the beast, cornered now, was about to bite.

Tweed fought back.

He paid off printers.

He sent aldermen to preach about "political sabotage" and "immigrant persecution."

He even tried to smear it as Irish prejudice, a patriotic veneer over the stench of theft.

But *The Times* didn't back down.

Then came **Thomas Nast**.

His cartoons in *Harper's Weekly*, Tweed as a bloated vulture devouring coins, the courthouse dripping with blood, sealed the verdict in public opinion.

No speech could erase those images: Tweed as a king, a leech, a cannibal.

October 27, 1871.

William M. Tweed was arrested in his home.

The charge was fraud.

But it was really treason, against the city, against the people, against the very idea of a vote.

Crowley watched from across the street.

No one saw him.

He didn't blink.

He didn't breathe.

The great beast of Tammany Hall was being led away in cuffs.

But in his gut, Crowley knew,

this **wasn't** the end.

Tweed was just the face.

The gears still turned.

The machine still fed.

And men like *John Kelly*, quiet, pious, patient, were already waiting in the wings.

That night, Crowley sat alone in his room.

He lit a cigar, its ember glowing like a slow confession, and opened his red ledger.

The last name.

The last number.

The last receipt.

Then the blank pages that followed.

Dozens of them.

He stared at the empty space, the silence between ink and consequence.

He wasn't putting the book away.

Not yet.

He was just getting started.

Chapter 11
A Quiet War

May 1872, The Bronx

Mary O'Brien Crowley folded laundry with fingers that no longer shook,

but trembled somewhere deeper, quietly, privately,

in the place where she kept her fear.

The apartment off 144th Street was still modest, but no longer small.

It held more now.

More light.

More laughter.

More certainty.

Because she was no longer just Mary O'Brien.

She was Mary Agnes Crowley, wife to the Honorable David H. Crowley, United States Deputy Marshal.

The New York Times had printed it in bold beneath the society column:

"Hon. David H. Crowley, United States Deputy Marshal, was married in St. Mary's Church, Wednesday evening, to Miss Mary O'Brien, a belle of the East Side."

Crowley had watched her for months before their first real words.

They lived in the same tenement near Monroe Street, he on the third floor, she on the second.

She was five years his junior, the daughter of a carman, known on the block for her steady hands and sharper eyes.

He noticed her first in winter, scrubbing laundry in cold water, humming hymns through chapped lips.

It wasn't love at first sight.

It was respect at first sight.

By summer 1871, as Crowley slipped deeper into his investigation of Tweed, she had begun leaving extra bread on the steps, never asking questions when his boots came home bloodied.

He offered quiet thanks.

She offered quieter comfort.

Their romance grew in the stillness between storms.

Now, in May 1872, beneath the high vaults of St. Mary's Church, they were joined.

The pews were packed, men from the U.S. Marshal's Office in pressed coats, Republican ward officials from the Seventh, Tenth, Eleventh, and Thirteenth. Even Bliss had cleaned up and stood as witness, whispering before the vows:

"You finally arrested someone permanent."

Afterward, there was music, dancing, and bourbon in the back hall.

Mary wore blue ribbons and shook hands with men who had once tried to ruin her husband.

Crowley smiled more that night than he had in a year.

But beneath the laughter, the city still hummed, grimy, glorious, and unforgiving.

The next morning, the war resumed.

Bliss arrived with apples and bad news.

"Tweed's grip is slipping," he said, setting his hat on the table, "but Kelly's already moving pieces. David's in deeper now. They know it."

Mary poured tea, her voice steady.

"Then we'll move quieter."

She said it with the steel of a woman who understood she was no longer just a wife.

She was a firewall.

A partner.

A keeper of the ledger behind the ledger.

That night, as David hung his coat near the stove, she pressed her hand gently to the sleeve.

The ink hadn't vanished.

But it didn't scare her anymore.

Outside, the city stirred.

Inside, Mary held the storm at bay.

Because now, they were one.

And war, true war, was never fought alone.

Chapter 12
The Election of Ghosts

November 5, 1872, New York City

The night air held no forgiveness.

A cold wind knifed through Union Square, stirring up mist beneath the gas lamps.

Under that haze, the city felt like a stage, one where the lead had fallen, but the villain still lingered behind the curtain.

The mayoral election had been a loss for Tammany. Reformist William Frederick Havemeyer, running on a Republican platform, had claimed victory and would take office in January.

But Crowley knew better.

Defeat didn't mean collapse. It meant adaptation.

Tammany's body might have gone down, but its roots still pulsed beneath the streets, fed by influence, bloodlines, and fear.

He followed the trail of ballots through dim corridors and damp stairwells.

Each polling hall reeked of ink, whiskey, and deception.

Clerks moved like automatons, extracting ghost votes with mechanical precision. Ward captains loitered in doorframes, their smiles lacquered and hollow in the lamplight.

At the Seventh Ward polling station, Crowley's patience thinned to a thread.

He approached the counter, his hand closing around a wad of folded slips in his coat pocket, prepared names, all long gone, all once recorded in the ledger he'd hidden near the stove.

He spoke the first name quietly, deliberately:

"Patrick Malloy."

The clerk's pen froze mid-air.

Eyes flicked up.

"He, " the man stammered, "he's been dead since spring."

Silence fell like a hammer.

Every head turned.

Then Mulligan, the foreman, fat-faced, red-eyed, and smiling too easily, stepped forward.

"Close kin, ain't that right?" he said. "Let the boy honor the family."

The clerk hesitated, swallowed, and slid the ballot through.

Crowley felt the shift in the air, the subtle awareness, the quiet fear.

The machine had noticed him.

He didn't wait to see the rest of the ballots fall.

He slipped into the fog outside, disappearing into the smoke and noise of the city.

Back in his room above the Cherry Street stable, he lit a single lamp.

He pulled the slips from his pocket, precinct names, clerk initials, ward captains, and held them near the flame.

Under the heat, the invisible ink flared into view, revealing ghostly handwriting scorched into paper.

Names of the dead.

Votes of the vanished.

He stared at the mirror above his desk.

His reflection wavered in the lamplight, haunted, divided.

Not triumphant.

Not clean.

Just tired.

Tammany had lost the election.

But they were still winning the war.

Outside, the crowd roared for revival, men shouting about reform, about clean government, about sweeping the streets of corruption.

But in the shadows, John Kelly was already rebuilding.

The new boss whispered into ears, thumbed through ward lists, and reshaped the city precinct by precinct.

The machine might have lost its banner, but not its hunger.

Every captain, every clerk, every ghost vote would soon find a new allegiance.

Lost elections are best survived quietly, Kelly thought. Then hit harder.

Crowley traced his fingers over the ink-burned names.

He imagined a slow reckoning, a single ledger that would outlast the men who thought themselves immortal.

Outside, they celebrated reform.

Inside, Crowley made plans.

Because the ghosts had voted.

But the living,

not silent anymore,

still remembered.

Chapter 13
The Narrowing

November 6, 1872 – The Bronx & Lower Manhattan

The morning after the election tasted like ash.

City papers shouted reform from every corner stall.

Havemeyer Wins!

Tweed's *Legacy Buried by the People!*

It sounded righteous.

Clean.

A new day.

But David Crowley didn't believe in new days.

Not in New York.

Not with John Kelly watching from behind the altar.

He sat at the kitchen table, both hands wrapped around a chipped mug of coffee.

The stove hissed softly.

And Mary, Mary stood behind him, her palms resting on his shoulders.

"You did what you could," she whispered.

Crowley didn't answer.

He had walked with ghosts.

Watched them vote.

Touched the levers of power as they clicked beneath dead hands.

And now Kelly, the priest-faced executioner, was taking the machine for his own.

By mid-morning, Bliss arrived.

No disguise this time.

He was too tired to pretend.

He dropped his coat on the hook, eyes hollow but sharp.

"Kelly didn't lose," he said flatly. "He just changed clothes. You hit him. He ducked. Now he's coiled."

Crowley nodded once.

"The mayor's house may be clean," Bliss continued, "but the streets still belong to him."

They spoke in low tones while Mary washed dishes in the corner, pretending not to listen, and hearing every word.

Kelly was already replacing precinct captains.

The Seventh Ward headquarters had a new lock.

A foreman from the Eleventh had turned up face-down in Gowanus Creek.

Quiet messages, wrapped in red.

That night, after the children had gone to bed, Mary brought out the ledger.

Not the main one, the backup.

The one she kept beneath the false bottom of the linen drawer.

Crowley looked at it in silence.

"You shouldn't have touched it," he said.

She arched an eyebrow.

"You shouldn't have left it where I could find it."

He exhaled, long, slow.

She sat beside him and opened the cover.

"Your hand shakes when you write now," she murmured. "I'll help."

He met her gaze, eyes rimmed with fatigue.

"This gets darker from here."

Mary nodded.

"Then we move with it. Together."

Across the river, John Kelly lit a cigar with the morning headlines.

The papers celebrated Havemeyer.

Kelly wasn't worried.

Reformers made speeches.

Tammany made deals.

He already had new men in place, Irish, educated, loyal.

Not Tweed's kind.

His kind.

One name still remained on his desk:

David Crowley.

He underlined it once.

And poured himself a drink.

Chapter 14
A New Badge, A New War

December 1872, Washington, D.C. & New York City

By twenty-seven, David Crowley had lived the kind of life that wore out other men by fifty.

He had charged up Cemetery Hill with the 69th New York, bleeding beside brothers who'd never see another sunrise. He'd knelt through midnight masses that masked rebel councils and hunted conspirators who cloaked treason in patriotism. He'd survived the Fenian infiltration by living inside a lie so deep it still echoed in his bones.

So when the envelope arrived, hand-delivered, unsigned, its only seal a crimson wax imprint cracked like dried blood, he didn't hesitate.

He packed light. Always had. A pistol slid into its worn leather holster, the ledger into a false-bottomed satchel. No goodbyes. No note to Mary Agnes. Just a train ticket and silence.

He didn't know who summoned him.

He already knew why.

Washington in December was grey steel and bitter wind. The streets of power buzzed with formality, but Crowley knew better. He knew how many monsters wore waistcoats and smiled for newspapers. The real war wasn't fought on battlefields anymore.

It was fought in boardrooms, backrooms, and ballot boxes.

And now, apparently, inside the Treasury.

He climbed the marble steps, boots echoing across cold stone. Inside, everything hummed, polished brass lamps, the smell of ink and damp paper, the hurried scurry of men who moved as if time itself were chasing them.

Near the grand staircase, a man waited: tall, cadaver-thin, in a brown suit that fit like a second skin.

"Inspector Jonathan Hale," the man said. "You're Crowley."

Crowley nodded without speaking. Hale didn't need confirmation.

"I'll be your contact," Hale said. "Informally, of course. Officially, "

"I don't exist," Crowley finished.

Hale handed over a folder. Thin. Worn. Edges curled as if it had been read and reread by too many nervous hands. One word was scrawled on the cover in fading graphite: **TAMMANY.**

"You know the name?" Hale asked.

"Everyone does," Crowley said.

What he meant was: *I've seen the rot under the paint. I've smelled it in alleyways and* heard *it* in the slurred confessions of *drunk aldermen. Tammany* isn't just *a name. It's a disease.*

Hale's voice dropped. "They're bleeding the Treasury dry. Ghost payrolls. Phantom land deals. Fictitious municipal bonds bought by banks that somehow always end up holding real cash. It starts in New York."

"And ends here," Crowley said.

Hale nodded. "In campaign funds. In committee appointments. In judges who suddenly retire wealthy."

Crowley flipped through the folder. No photographs, just account ledgers, initials, and symbols. Transfers across banks in Montreal, Charleston, and Havana. A coded spider web.

"You want me to track it," he said.

"To its source," Hale replied. "Then disappear again."

"No confrontation?"

"Not yet. The man orchestrating this isn't in New York. He's two floors above us, sitting behind a mahogany desk, wearing a flag pin and shaking hands with senators."

Crowley's silence wasn't agreement. It was commitment. He was already in.

A week later, Crowley found himself in a smoke-filled office above a warehouse in Trenton. A man from the Marshals Service, no name, just a coat and a voice, slid a flat tin badge across the desk:

United States Marshal

Temporary Duty , Internal Assignment

"Cover identity," the man said. "Effective immediately. You'll be assigned as a sergeant in the New York City Police Department. Officially, you're assisting on political corruption enforcement. Unofficially, you're hunting shadows."

Crowley turned the badge in his hand. It was unpolished. Cold. Real.

"There's rot in the city," the man continued. "And we need a man who's already been in the dark. Who won't blink when things get ugly. You come highly recommended."

That recommendation came from George Bliss Jr. Once Crowley's handler during the Fenian infiltration, now something else, something bigger. Bliss had never said exactly who he worked for. Only that he "answered upward."

Bliss had been the only man to ever ask Crowley *why* he kept doing this work, not *how*, not *when*, but *why*. Crowley had answered honestly.

"Because the men I buried never had a choice. I do."

George Bliss Jr., U.S. Attorney for the Southern District of New York, appointed by President Ulysses S. Grant in December 1872 and serving until January 24, 1877, had placed a hand on his shoulder that night: firm, not friendly.

"This next one's going to get personal," Bliss warned. "Tammany doesn't kill you all at once. It eats your name. Your honor. Your family. Piece by piece."

"I can take it," Crowley said.

"You better. Because if we miss, they don't just bury us. They promote the man who does it."

Now, in New York City, Crowley stood beneath the gas lamps of Mulberry Street in a borrowed uniform, the badge heavy on his chest.

Sergeant David Crowley, NYPD.

A ghost with a badge and a target painted on his back.

He wasn't there to make arrests. Not yet. He was there to *listen*, to watch the precinct captains who played poker with ward bosses, to map the judges who bought verdicts like cigars, to sit in taverns where Tammany's street soldiers passed envelopes across greasy tables.

To find the thread that would unravel the whole damn machine.

And when it was ready?

He would pull it.

Hard.

Chapter 15
The Captain's Game

January 1873 – Delancey Street, Lower East Side

The badge wasn't the danger.

The silence was.

Crowley's first day came without applause, no handshake, no ceremony. Just a damp wool coat, a desk shoved into the back corner of the 7th Precinct, and a suspicious glance from every man in the room.

He wasn't one of them, and they all knew it.

But no one said a word. They watched. He watched harder.

The 7th Precinct was a spider's web, everything connected to something else: missing evidence, evaporated charges, suspects who vanished between alley and courtroom.

At the center of it all stood Captain Owen Malley, tall, mustached, granite-faced. Malley didn't give orders. He gave favors. Promotions. Inside tips. Immunity. All of it funneled through him, and, by extension, through Tammany Hall.

Crowley played it careful.

He took the beats nobody wanted: Chinatown after dark. The Bowery on Sundays.

He broke up bar fights. Hauled drunks. Tipped his cap. Kept his mouth shut.

On the thirteenth day of the new year, his world changed.

He came off patrol to find Bliss waiting near the precinct gates. Bliss didn't speak, just handed over a folded clipping from *The New York Times*:

Born Wednesday evening to Mr. and Mrs. David H. Crowley, a son: David Jr. Mother and child are well.

Crowley read it three times before the chill in his spine gave way to something deeper. Real. Immovable.

He had a son.

He had a reason.

That night, he stood beside Mary's bed at St. Mary's Infirmary, watching her cradle a sleeping bundle of linen and promise. She looked up with tired eyes but managed a smile.

"His fists were clenched," she said. "Just like yours."

Crowley sat. Held the boy.

And for a moment, just a moment, the war outside faded.

Two days later, the war returned.

He was pulled from his beat early and ordered to Captain Malley's office.

Malley didn't look up.

"You Irish?"

"Cork."

"You fought?"

"Sixty-Ninth. Gettysburg. Antietam."

Malley finally raised his eyes.

"Good. Boys respect blood. You'll be doing collections this week."

"Collections?"

"Widows and Orphans Fund," Malley said flatly. "Tenements. Saloons. Right envelopes. Right hands."

Crowley didn't blink.

"Uniform or plainclothes?"

Malley smiled thinly.

"Badge out. Always better when they see who owns them."

That night, Crowley mapped the route. Six stops. Four were Tammany fronts, saloons stacked with loyalists, boarding houses used to register the dead.

At stop three, he was handed an envelope with cash, and a folded slip of paper:

Five names. Five precinct numbers. Ghost votes and payroll fraud.

It was the crack in the wall.

Over the next two weeks, he followed the rot:

Pay envelopes delivered to ghost cops.

A tailor on Delancey printing counterfeit ballots.

Malley's men routing election money through phantom construction jobs.

He logged every name. Every dollar. Every date.

Then came Connor Doyle.

Young. Smart. Curious. Dangerous.

"You're not what you look like," Doyle said one morning.

Crowley didn't deny it.

"I found thirty-seven names on the 12th Ward rolls tied to an alley. No building. No beds."

"Keep digging," Crowley said. "But don't talk."

"Are you part of something?"

"No," Crowley said. "I'm what shows up when something breaks."

That night, he sent his first coded dispatch to Bliss, folded into a shipping manifest:

Tammany deep inside 7th Precinct. Malley key. Pattern confirmed. Watch Doyle. Possible ally.

The reply came three days later, baked into a loaf from a Delancey Street bakery:

Good. Keep going. When it's time, we burn it clean. , GB

Then the air shifted.

One night, he found his lock picked. Nothing missing, just... rearranged.

Another night, his beat changed. New patrol through Five Points. Blind corners. No backup.

Someone was watching.

Someone inside the precinct was about to find out exactly who Sergeant Crowley really was.

And now, he had more to protect than ever.

Chapter 16
The Envelope That Vanished

February 1873 – 7th Precinct, New York City

It was never about the money.

Not really.

It was about the message.

So when one envelope, just one, failed to show on Malley's desk that Thursday morning, the precinct didn't explode. It simmered. Whispers replaced greetings. Coffee cups clinked a little too sharply. A patrolman who usually joked with Crowley didn't meet his eye.

Crowley knew before the words were spoken.

The envelope hadn't been lost. It hadn't been stolen. It had been marked. Deliberately. A test.

And someone had failed.

He didn't wait to be summoned. He went to Malley.

The captain's office smelled of pipe smoke and damp wallpaper. Yellowed maps of the Five Points curled on the walls. A half-finished bottle of rye sat on a sideboard beside a pewter cup.

Malley didn't offer a seat.

"Sergeant," he said, tone flat, hands folded over his blotter. "Walk me through your collections on Grand Street."

Crowley stood still. Calm.

"There was a short at O'Grady's. Owner said he was light from the last take. Gave me half."

"Half," Malley echoed. "Did he mention why he reported a full payment this morning? Directly. To me."

Crowley blinked once. "No."

Malley rose and crossed to the sideboard, pouring rye slow and deliberate. He turned.

"I know who you are," he said quietly. "Not the uniform. You."

Crowley didn't answer.

"I've had men follow you. You think your routes change by accident? You think your reports go unread? You're not from here. You didn't come up through the chain. You landed. Like a brick."

Still, Crowley held his ground.

"And now an envelope disappears," Malley said. "First time in six years. And it's your route."

"You saying I took it?" Crowley asked, voice cold.

"I'm saying you've got too clean a coat for this mud," Malley said. "And the men are starting to ask why it doesn't stick to you."

He moved closer, close enough to smell the rye on his breath.

"Whatever game you're playing," he said, "you're not the first. The others didn't last. Some resigned. Some were transferred. One of them..." He sipped. "Went to retrieve his hat in the Hudson."

Crowley's jaw tensed. "That a warning?"

Malley smiled. "A favor."

Long silence. Then Crowley stepped forward, just enough.

"I've served this city. I've bled in fields while men like you sent telegrams and collected bribes. You want to threaten me, Captain? Fine. But if I fall, someone else picks up the badge. Someone worse."

"You think you're better than this place?" Malley asked, eyes narrowing.

"I think I remember what it was supposed to be."

Malley drained the glass and tossed it at the wall. It shattered with a sharp crack.

"Get out of my office," he said. "While you still have the coat."

Crowley turned to the door, paused.

"Next time you have me followed," he said, "tell them to wear different boots. Same ones three days in a row? That's sloppy."

Malley said nothing. But Crowley didn't need him to.

That night, Crowley didn't go home. He went to Doyle.

Connor Doyle opened his tenement door with a Colt in his hand, saw Crowley, and lowered it slowly.

"You ready to choose a side?" Crowley asked.

Doyle's eyes flicked to the hallway. "Is there still time?"

"Barely," Crowley said. "But if you help, if you stay sharp, we can pull this thing down to the bricks."

Doyle nodded.

"Who do we go after first?" he asked.

Crowley didn't hesitate.

"Malley."

Chapter 17
The Price of Loyalty

February 1873 – East Village, 7th Precinct

It started with a bottle of rye and a lie.

Malley didn't trust people. He trusted patterns, routines and movement that matched expectation. That was the only thing that ever lulled men like him into blinking. So Crowley gave him a pattern.

Three weeks of obedience. Clean collections. Quiet nights. A few strategic nods to Connor Doyle, nothing overt. Crowley kept his head down, his voice even, his paperwork precise. He even complimented Malley on a recent raid, just enough to seed comfort.

Then came the bait.

The meeting was staged in a closed billiard parlor on Canal Street, late Sunday evening. Doyle played his part well: anxious, new, hungry. Crowley walked in with an envelope, fat, folded, stained just enough to look dirty, real.

"I need this to get to the captain," he said, sliding it across the table to Doyle. "He's expecting it."

"What is it?"

"A gratuity," Crowley said. "From a friend of a friend who's tired of health inspectors visiting his bakery."

Doyle frowned. "Is this how it's done?"

"Don't ask questions. Just deliver it."

Doyle palmed the envelope, nodded once, and left through the back alley.

The second he was gone, Crowley stepped into the next room, where George Bliss Jr. waited with two Treasury men and a stenographer.

They had witnesses. The marked bills. The serial numbers recorded. The bribe documented in six different hands before it ever left the table.

Now they needed the reaction.

Doyle entered Malley's office the next morning and handed over the envelope like a nervous altar boy. The captain didn't look at it. He didn't open it.

He only said, "Tell Crowley it was light."

That was the tell.

The envelope had contained exactly five hundred dollars in marked bills, more than any collection that month. Malley knew it wasn't real. The pattern had broken. Crowley had him.

That night, Malley called a meeting, not at the precinct (too exposed), but in the back room of O'Rourke's Tavern, under the elevated rail line, where you couldn't hear your own thoughts.

Crowley was already inside, in the shadows, watching.

Malley entered with two men, one Doyle knew from the docks, the other a Tammany ward captain. Drinks were poured.

Then Malley said it: "Crowley's not ours. He's planted. Bliss's man. Maybe more."

The room stilled.

"He made a mistake," Malley continued. "That envelope wasn't for me. It was a leash."

"What do we do?" the ward captain asked.

Malley leaned back. "We cut the dog loose."

Doyle paled.

Crowley had heard enough. He stepped from the shadows like a priest at judgment.

"No," he said. "You burn with the leash."

Malley went for his gun. Doyle was faster, the revolver clattered to the floor. Malley lunged, wild and desperate, then froze as George Bliss Jr. himself stepped in behind Crowley, flanked by federal marshals.

"The room has witnesses," Bliss said. "The money's marked. The serials are on record. This is a federal matter."

Malley stared at Crowley. "You think this city will thank you?" he hissed. "You think they care about justice? They want gas lamps and streetcars and cheap bread. They don't care how it gets there."

Crowley stepped forward. "They don't yet. But they will."

Malley was arrested on counts of conspiracy, bribery, and falsifying payroll ledgers. More charges would follow. Doyle's testimony held. The documented money and the stenographer's transcript held.

But Tammany didn't shriek. It smiled.

Men like Tweed didn't flinch when lieutenants fell; they hired new ones. Bliss knew it. Crowley knew it.

"This isn't the top," George Bliss Jr. said later. "Malley was a rung. We need the architect."

Crowley nodded.

"I know where to find him."

Chapter 18
The Marble Curtain

March 1873– The Tweed Courthouse, Chambers Street

The new courthouse on Chambers Street was supposed to be the crown jewel of New York justice. Instead it was a mausoleum for the law, built on stolen money, forged ledgers, and silence.

Outside: white marble, imperial columns. Inside: old varnish, sweat, and the smell of expensive cigars. The stairwells echoed with bailiffs' boots and the whispered deals of men who never saw a courtroom unless they were naming a judge.

Crowley had been inside before. But never like this. Now he wasn't chasing one corrupt cop or one forged ballot. He was hunting something bigger: a network. The system behind the system.

It started with a name George Bliss Jr. had given him: Isaiah Pulford, the city's deputy comptroller. A bookkeeper by trade. A gatekeeper by design. Pulford handled the court-construction invoices, stone shipments that never arrived, laborers who never worked, railings charged four times over.

Crowley followed him. Twice a week Pulford left the courthouse just after dusk, walked east down Chambers, and slipped into a nondescript brick building that called itself the Civic Preservation Society.

Crowley went in after him one rainy Tuesday night.

What he found wasn't civic. It was a ledger den, three men working under gaslight beside stacks of double books: one for the city, one for the real buyers. Contractors paid kickbacks to Tammany for every approved invoice. Pulford took a cut. The rest went into an account marked Construction Contingency, code for election funds.

Crowley photographed pages with a small field camera supplied by the Treasury. He smuggled one receipt out inside his coat lining, a thirty-foot iron railing that had been "purchased" six separate times, each with a new invoice number and a false delivery signature.

Next he turned his sights on Judge Albert Tilden, appointed by Tweed, presiding over fraud indictments tied to city contracts. Tilden hadn't dismissed every case. Just the important ones.

Crowley dug through financial disclosures quietly obtained through a sympathetic clerk. No smoking gun at first, until he checked property records. Tilden's brother-in-law had purchased a Gramercy Park brownstone six weeks after Tilden dismissed an injunction against the City Board of Works. The deed was under a shell company, Thistle & Brace, Ltd. The signature traced back to a notary who worked for Pulford. The circle tightened.

The next link came from Doyle. He'd embedded himself with the night bailiff crew, acting as the eyes and ears between judges' chambers and the fixers who met them after hours. One night Doyle followed a junior clerk from Tilden's office to a cigar shop near the Battery. The clerk emerged with a small wrapped parcel and entered the Knickerbocker Bank through a freight door. Doyle bribed the porter with a silver dollar and watched. The clerk deposited the parcel in a private box registered to A. Turney, an alias George Bliss later confirmed belonged to Peter Sweeny, Tweed's chief legal advisor.

Crowley now had:

invoices laundered through Pulford;

real-estate payoffs tied to Judge Tilden;

bank transactions flowing to Tammany leadership.

But he needed a linchpin.

He found it in a place most men ignored: mass. Mrs. Margaret Gildea, a widowed court stenographer whose son had died of yellow fever the year before, had been overlooked by everyone but Crowley. He spoke with her after service, listened, earned her trust. She handed him what she ought not to have kept, transcripts from Judge Tilden's private chambers: preliminary hearings that never reached the public docket. Conversations between judge and city lawyers about "pre-clearing" defenses. One referenced a strategy session with "the Old Man."

Tweed.

By April, Crowley had enough for George Bliss Jr. to move. The case file was a monster, three inches thick, bound with twine, heavy with names that reached from contractors to federal officeholders. Bliss reviewed it in silence. When he finished, he lit a cigar.

"They'll deny everything," he said. "And the press? Half of them are on the payroll."

"I know," Crowley said.

"And if this leaks before we strike, someone ends up in the East River. Might be you."

"I know that too."

Bliss leaned forward.

"This is the biggest case we've ever touched, David. You sure you're ready to light the fuse?"

Crowley stood.

"It's already burning."

Chapter 19
The Whisper War

April 1873...– New York City

Justice couldn't come loud.

Not yet.

This was a war of whispers.

The file was sealed, triple-wrapped in oilcloth and locked inside a Treasury safehouse disguised as a hatmaker's shop on Bleecker Street. Only three men had seen its full contents: Crowley, George Bliss Jr., and a federal auditor who now traveled with an armed escort.

Bliss called it The Chain.

"If we strike too early," he warned, "they'll cut it apart and burn what's left. We move only when the full weight lands in one place. One blow. No leaks. No mercy."

But Tammany already knew.

Not everything, not yet. But enough. Enough to feel the heat.

It began with surveillance.

Crowley noticed first at St. Patrick's Cathedral, a man in a derby two pews back. Didn't take communion. Didn't cross himself. Left when Crowley did.

Then came the tap at Doyle's window in the middle of the night, no sound, just a calling card on the sill:

You can still walk away.

The next day, Doyle's younger brother, a schoolteacher, was accused of indecent conduct. No evidence. No hearing. His teaching certificate simply disappeared into "processing."

And then the reporter.

James Houghton, Herald staff writer and reformist, contacted Crowley through an anonymous letter drop. Said he had photographs, proof of Tweed's men exchanging cash inside the courthouse vault.

He never made the meeting.

His body washed up in the East River the next morning. No wallet. No camera.

No headline.

Inside the precinct, Malley's absence hadn't cleansed the rot, it only shifted it. Captain Reynard Pike, a Tammany loyalist with polished boots and a softer tone, took over the 8th. He invited Crowley for a drink the first week. Crowley declined.

That same week, his patrol schedule changed again, graveyard shift in Hell's Kitchen. Twice he was redirected to "disturbances" that turned into ambushes. The second time, he crawled out with a broken rib and a knife wound along his left hip.

Bliss visited him two days later in a Bronx boarding house where Crowley lay stitched, bandaged, and half-drunk on laudanum.

"We can pull you out," Bliss said. "Call it in. Let the papers take it."

"No," Crowley grunted. "Not yet. They're circling. That means they're scared."

Bliss frowned. "You're walking the line between brave and dead."

Crowley lit a cigarette with shaking fingers. "Tell me where the line ends," he muttered, "and I'll stop walking."

Meanwhile, The Chain tightened.

Doyle secured a copy of a construction invoice bearing three signatures, all forged versions of a retired city clerk's name. Bliss traced the handwriting to Cornelius McHale, a former contractor with deep Tammany ties, now running a "consulting firm" above a Fifth Avenue pharmacy.

Crowley confronted him in the back of a cigar parlor.

"You think I give a damn about ink and dates?" McHale scoffed. "Tweed runs this city with bricks and blood. He doesn't need lawyers. He needs loyalty."

Crowley placed a photograph on the table, Houghton's last image, salvaged from a half-developed plate in a pawnshop camera.

It showed McHale holding a cash satchel outside the courthouse vault.

"You're dead either way," Crowley said. "Work with us, you might see daylight."

McHale paled.

"I want immunity."

"You'll get it," Crowley said. "If you live that long."

But immunity took time.

So Crowley stayed buried in shadows. Each night he changed coats and routes, slept in different rooms, trusted no one. Still, he felt it. The city itself had grown quieter. People spoke in murmurs. Windows cracked open only halfway. Doors waited for triple knocks and whispered names.

It was as if everyone knew something was coming.

They just didn't know whose side it would land on.

The final whisper came from a messenger boy, no older than eleven, cap askew, eyes darting. He passed Crowley a sealed envelope and vanished into the fog before he could ask who sent it.

Inside: a single sheet of parchment.

No greeting. No signature. Only a line, handwritten in a delicate slant:

"The axe forgets, but the tree remembers."

Crowley folded the note. Struck a match. Watched it burn to ash in the alley wind.

Then he turned toward the courthouse.

It was time to finish The Chain.

Chapter 20
The Turn

New York City, Secret Holding Location

They moved Cornelius McHale under cover of darkness.

Three Treasury agents, two decoy carriages, and a night rain that washed the streets clean of curious eyes. Crowley watched from a corner window of the safehouse in Brooklyn Heights as the last lantern was doused. Inside, the rooms were cold, windowless, and wired.

McHale sat at a table in a rumpled vest, wet from nerves. His hands trembled just enough to betray the mask he tried to wear.

"You've got no idea what they'll do to me," he said, voice fraying. "They don't *threaten*. They *erase*."

Crowley poured two coffees from a tin kettle and slid one across the table.

"You're already erased, Cornelius. You just haven't accepted it yet."

McHale laughed bitterly. "You think Bliss can protect me? You think a courtroom matters when Sweeny buys judges like cigars?"

Crowley leaned in. "You're right. The law won't save you."

That stopped him. Crowley tapped the tabletop. "But you might."

The interrogation wasn't physical. It didn't need to be. Crowley had **leverage**: a name, a date, a photograph. He didn't ask questions so much as answer them before McHale could open his mouth, listed payments, tied bank transactions to shell companies, recited the name of McHale's mistress in Albany.

"You've been laundering money through city contracts since '69," Crowley said. "You padded the courthouse build. The Second Avenue bridge. You signed false vouchers and shipped kickbacks to an account at Metropolitan Trust under your second wife's name."

McHale froze. "I never told anyone about that account."

"You didn't need to," Crowley said. "You wrote it down once, three years ago, on a shipment manifest for limestone. Treasury reconstructed the imprint from the blotter page."

McHale stared. Then he broke.

At sunrise, George Bliss Jr. arrived, coat damp, gloves off.

"You ready?" he asked, nodding to McHale.

"He's talking," Crowley said. Bliss's face didn't relax.

"We don't have long. Sweeny knows he's missing. Tweed will throw bodies at us until we bleed him dry or bury him ourselves."

McHale looked up. "I want my family moved. My boy's at Saint Ignatius. My wife thinks I'm in Albany on bidding."

"You get us everything," Bliss said, "and they'll be gone before sundown."

That day, McHale began naming names.

Peter Sweeny, legal fixer and bagman. **Isaiah Pulford**, the deputy comptroller who split kickbacks three ways: one for himself, one for Tammany, one for quiet judges. **Judge Albert Tilden**, dismissed injunctions in exchange for land deeds recorded under his brother-in-law's name. Even **Mayor A. Oakey Hall** appeared, once or twice, in correspondence marked with the codename *"Canary."*

They transcribed for twelve hours straight. Crowley had a team comparing McHale's handwriting against invoices from the courthouse vault. One matched: a check authorization for $147,000 to a contractor that never existed.

By nightfall, Crowley had enough to begin a **grand-jury** file.

But McHale wasn't finished. He leaned forward, voice a whisper. "There's one more name."

"Go on."

McHale looked haunted. "Tweed isn't the spider. He's the web. There's a hand behind the curtain, somebody in the State Assembly who kills investigations before they start."

"Who?" Bliss asked.

"I never met him. They call him *the Bookkeeper*. He manages the political ledger. Allocates silence. Even Tweed answers to him."

Bliss and Crowley exchanged a look: a second tier. A *deeper* ring. The architecture of corruption ran through Albany, and into Washington.

"We'll take this to the grand jury. Quietly. No headlines yet. Let them think we're still guessing," Bliss said.

Crowley nodded. "We'll need to move McHale again. Get his family out before Sweeny finds them."

Bliss glanced back at the contractor, drained, pale, but finally telling the truth. "I'll handle the family," he said. "You handle the rest."

Crowley cracked his knuckles. "Oh, I will."

That night, a coded telegraph went **to Albany.** Crowley didn't know who sent it. But the wire bore six words:

"The stone is rolling. Prepare disposal."

Chapter 21
Twelve Stones

May 1873 – Southern District Courthouse, New York City

The jury box was nothing like the ones in paintings.

No heroic lighting. No majestic scales etched in marble. Just twelve men seated in a paneled room that smelled of dust, sweat, and aged varnish, one cracked window, three sputtering oil lamps, and a bailiff who coughed too often.

They were farmers, bankers, retired tradesmen, white-bearded, white-knuckled, unsure why they'd been summoned with no docket notice, no press, no brass-buttoned pageantry. That was the point.

George Bliss Jr. stood at the front, quiet, unblinking.

Behind him on the oak table sat a stack of files six inches high. Crowley stood off to the side in plainclothes, arms crossed, face unreadable.

"Gentlemen," Bliss said, "you are not here for a criminal trial."

He let that silence sit.

"You are here for a reckoning."

For the first hour the grand jury didn't know what to make of it. This was not a body. Not a single theft. It was a system, a perfectly engineered machine for laundering public wealth into private power.

Bliss walked them through it slowly, carefully, brick by brick: invoice fraud, bond theft, forged payrolls, phantom workers, land swaps between city boards and shell companies, contracts that paid for materials that never arrived, and judges who signed off on it all.

And then came Cornelius McHale. Testifying under heavy guard, he laid out the scheme like a man unburdening a mortal sin, names, times, numbers, copies of handwritten orders. He named Pulford, Tilden, Sweeny, and implicated Tweed directly in two decisions tied to courthouse funding approvals. He even told them about the safehouse vault beneath the Union Trust building, where bribe ledgers were kept along with key contracts.

When McHale finished, one juror, an old dock foreman, set his hands flat on the table and said, simply, "You're telling us the whole city's been stolen. Not once. Every day."

Bliss nodded. "Yes. And now we need to take it back."

Outside the grand jury chamber the city didn't know. Not yet. But Tammany did. They could smell the shift. Their runners reported Pulford missing, McHale vanished, reporters asking new questions, police precincts growing quiet.

Tweed convened a private council at Delmonico's, eight men, wine set down on linen, calculation where panic might have been. "Crowley," Peter Sweeny said, voice tight. "That's the one."

Tweed tapped his fork on the table. "I've met him. Once. Didn't like his eyes."

Bliss and Crowley knew they were running out of time.

By the second day one juror's wife received a note warning her to "keep her husband home for his own safety." On the third day the courthouse janitor was found beaten in the basement, nothing taken, a message left in bruises.

The jury could not be moved. Not now. Bliss kept them guarded, night escorts, unmarked carriages, each man relocated every evening to a new address. Crowley did not sleep. He met Doyle twice a day, re-verified signatures, cross-referenced deposits. No cracks. No excuses.

The moment they presented evidence on Tweed it had to land like a dropped anvil.

On the fifth day Crowley entered the courthouse with two case files and a pistol at his waistband. He passed a note to Bliss:

Sweeny knows. They're preparing a counter-strike, press disinformation, character attacks. Maybe worse.

Bliss read it, folded it, burned it in a lamp. "I want indictments within the week," he said. "We strike before they do."

Crowley nodded. "Then we bring them all down."

Back in the grand jury room Bliss dropped a final folder on the table. Inside: bank slips, contract swaps, and a coded letter signed by A. Oakey Hall, the mayor himself. It was no longer about one man. It was the whole damn city.

The fuse was almost gone.

Chapter 22
Smoke and Mirrors

May–June 1873 – New York City

It began on page three of the New York Herald, under the headline:

"Is Sergeant Crowley a Spy or a Scoundrel?"

No byline. Just an anonymous column citing "sources close to City Hall," questioning Crowley's sudden rise, his military record, and his presence in multiple "unrelated investigations." It didn't call him a criminal.

It did something worse.

It called him untrustworthy.

A man with no past. No station. A ghost in a badge.

By week's end, the Evening Telegram echoed the smear:

"Secret Policeman or Political Agent?"

Then came the broadsides, flyers nailed to precinct doors, saloons, and church steps:

- *"Who is David Crowley really working for?"*
- *"Answer to no one = answer to anyone."*
- *"One man's crusade is another man's cover-up."*

They plastered his face with a distorted sketch. Called him Bliss's stooge. Whispered about a romantic entanglement with a known Fenian informant, Bridget Cahill's name rising again like a ghost from the grave.

Tweed's machine had shifted into full gear.

They couldn't stop the grand jury.

So they went after the man building it.

Crowley expected it. So did Bliss.

"It's a diversion," Bliss said, reading the Times editorial with a disgusted curl of the lip. "They're softening the ground. Trying to make it easier for the public to believe you're the criminal when we name the real one."

Crowley sat by the window, jaw tight, watching a man in a bowler linger too long beneath the lamppost.

"You know what they say about blood in the water," Crowley muttered.

Bliss nodded. "Yeah. It's never the sharks that get you. It's the crowd that shows up to watch."

But the grand jury didn't stop.

June 6, 1873 , The Indictment Landed Like a Thunderclap.

William M. Tweed, a.k.a. *"Boss" Tweed*

Isaiah Pulford, Comptroller

Peter B. Sweeny, Legal Counsel

Judge Albert Tilden

Richard Connolly, Auditor General

Twenty counts of Grand Larceny, Official Malfeasance, Conspiracy to Defraud, and Obstruction of Justice.

The news broke like a dam. Crowds flooded Chambers Street. Some cheered. Some spat. Some just stared, unsure if what they witnessed was justice or just another show.

The *Times*, finally off its leash, ran the headline full width:

"THE BOSS IN CHAINS, TWEED INDICTED BY GRAND JURY."

Tweed turned himself in, flanked by marshals. He arrived in a silk waistcoat and a smile, waving to the crowd. Called it a misunderstanding. Behind him, Connolly wept. Sweeny fled the country.

Crowley watched from the courthouse shadows.

He didn't smile.

This wasn't over.

The trial was set for **October**.

In the months that followed, Tammany tried everything:

- Challenged the jury pool for bias.
- Claimed the evidence was "Federal intrusion."
- Accused Bliss of political vendetta.
- Accused Crowley of falsifying testimony to settle "old army grudges."

None of it stuck.

Because McHale held firm.

Because the documents couldn't be denied.

Because the city, finally, *wanted it to be true.*

Reformers who had stayed silent began stepping forward. Clerks. Contractors. Two former aldermen. The city had watched Tammany steal, lie, and bury men for years. But now the curtain had been pulled back.

And Crowley?

He kept working. Kept quiet. Moved like a man with unfinished business. Because there were still names in his ledger. Still judges on the bench. Still elections to rig.

The indictment was the first hammer blow.

But the wall hadn't fallen yet.

Chapter 23
The People's Case

October 1873 – Court of Oyer and Terminer, New York City

They said justice was blind. But in this courtroom, she was wearing spectacles, and she was *watching everything*.

The gallery was packed. Reporters from Boston, Philadelphia, even London elbowed for space. Reformers in stiff collars sat beside machine men with brass pins in their lapels. The press called it "The Trial of the Century."

But Crowley wasn't there to be seen.

He sat in the shadows beneath the gallery, one row behind the stenographers, plain coat, no badge, no recognition.

Just eyes.

Watching Boss Tweed take the stand for the first time.

The indictment carried 220 counts.

Only 60 were selected for trial.

The charges ranged from grand larceny to forgery, official misconduct, and conspiracy to defraud. The damage to the city exceeded $30 million, a staggering figure in a world where a skilled worker earned $500 a year.

Presiding was Judge Noah Davis, a man known for rigid formality and an almost heretical immunity to bribes. He'd already warned both sides: no theatrics, no politics, no mercy.

The prosecution was led by George Bliss Jr., crisp and clinical, with Wheeler Peckham at his side, a rising legal star with the patience of a surgeon.

But Tweed had his own weapon: David Dudley Field, brother of a Supreme Court Justice and a master of courtroom persuasion.

Bliss opened with a line from the city charter:

"The funds of this city belong to its people. Let this court show whether the people still have a voice."

Then came the evidence.

McHale's testimony was the first hammer blow. Structured. Damning. Unwavering.

He led the jury through the anatomy of theft, ledger fraud, contract padding, and the ghost machinery of the "Commissioners of Public Works."

Crowley watched from the shadows. McHale was pale, thinner, but composed. No man under protection wanted to be remembered, but McHale would be.

He pointed to the forged checks. The triple-billed invoices. The shell companies, *Americus Construction*, *Tweed & Co.*, *Garfield Pavement Supply*, all feeding the Ring's slush fund.

Then came the paper trail: checks endorsed by Richard Connolly, countersigned by ghost employees, deposited in accounts tied to Tweed's allies and relatives.

At one point, Bliss held up an invoice:

$12,000 for forty *chairs for the courthouse.*

A murmur rippled through the room.

"The defense claims they were custom," Bliss said. "The only thing custom was the theft."

Tweed's defense was classic misdirection.

Field painted Tweed as a man betrayed by his own subordinates. *Too* trusting, he said. *Too generous.* Connolly and Sweeny, he claimed, were the real villains.

Crowley almost laughed aloud.

It was the oldest trick in the book, absolve the boss, blame the lieutenants.

But it wasn't sticking.

The jurors weren't fools. They saw the checks. They saw the matching handwritings. They saw Tweed's signature on everything.

Then came the disruption.

Halfway through the third week, two jurors were offered bribes. One came forward. The other vanished for a day, returned shaken, silent. Judge Davis called it "a serious breach," but the trial continued.

Outside, the papers turned.

The *Times* called the trial "a referendum on the soul of the city."

The *Tribune* ran a sketch of Tweed beneath a headline:

"THE FACE OF GREED."

But not everyone wanted him to fall.

Crowley intercepted a note to a key witness, an offer of $5,000 and safe passage to Havana. He stopped it. But he knew others were coming.

Then, on November 19, 1873, the jury returned.

They had deliberated for eight days.

Deadlocked.

A mistrial.

Twelve men, ten for conviction, two against. Bribed, maybe. Bought, maybe not.

Crowley walked into the cold November wind feeling nothing.

Bliss caught up with him outside.

"We had him," Bliss muttered.

Crowley didn't look up. "We still do."

The DA refiled immediately.

A second trial convened within months, this time under heavier guard and tighter scrutiny. The city was paying attention now.

Crowley stayed away. He didn't need to be in the courtroom.

The fuse he'd lit months earlier had become a fire too big to stop.

November 1873 , Final Verdict:

Guilty on 204 counts.

Fined $12,750 and sentenced to 12 years in Ludlow Street Jail.

The punishment was more insult than justice. The fine was nothing. The time would shrink. But the machine had been pierced.

Tweed would die behind bars.

And Crowley knew this was only the first empire to fall.

The ledger in his coat pocket still held *other names.*

And New York still had too many shadows.

Chapter 24
The Smoke That Lingers

Winter 1873 – New York City

The city didn't erupt when Tweed was sentenced.

It exhaled.

For months, the courthouse had been a circus of headlines, sketches, and half-truths. But when the final verdict fell, there were no parades, no bells, just cold rain on iron streets.

David Crowley watched from a bench across from Ludlow Street Jail as the man who once ruled New York shuffled through the gate, head down, beard gray, coat soaked through.

William M. Tweed. The Boss.

Incarcerated on 204 counts.

Dead behind walls before the city even remembered how to forget him.

But Crowley didn't smile.

Because the real fight was only beginning.

The reformers rose like steam from a dying fire. They called themselves the Committee of Seventy, a coalition of newspaper men, civic reformers, lawyers, and bankers. Men with clean fingernails and loud speeches.

They lobbied for new elections, independent audits, and civil service exams to replace patronage. Even The New York Times, once cautious, turned crusader.

Laws changed. Budgets were reviewed. Appointments scrutinized.

But Crowley saw the cracks between the reforms.

For every corrupt official ousted, a quieter one stepped in, less greedy, more subtle. The city had shifted gears, not direction. Tammany wasn't dead. It had just learned to whisper instead of shout.

George Bliss was promoted, offered a federal judgeship. He declined.

Instead, he stayed on, investigating customs fraud, bank bribery, and the same rot in finer clothes.

He met Crowley one last time at a quiet corner table in the Union League Club.

"You saved the city," Bliss said.

"No," Crowley replied. "We just stopped it from bleeding long enough to bandage the wound."

Bliss studied him. "Come with me to Washington. Special Assignments. You'd have reach."

Crowley shook his head.

"I'm not done here."

He kept the red ledger. Still filled with names, some struck through, some underlined, some circled in black ink.

Some were still in office.

Some were already rising.

In the months that followed, he rooted out procurement fraud in the Dock Board, exposed ballot tampering in the 21st Ward, and worked behind the curtain, always one step ahead of the next fixer, the next whisper, the next envelope slid across a tavern table at dusk.

But there were quieter victories too.

New judges took the bench, men without debts.

Precincts saw new captains who wore their uniforms with pride, not fear.

And Connor Doyle, now Detective First Class, stayed sharp, and loyal.

The wind was shifting.

Not fast. Not enough. But it was real.

One evening in December, Crowley stood outside the Tweed Courthouse.

The building still loomed, white marble, polished windows, a monument to stolen wealth and twisted ambition. Children played on the steps. Vendors hawked roasted chestnuts at the curb. Life went on.

The courthouse had a new plaque now. It read:

Dedicated to the People of New York. A New Era of Justice.

Crowley smiled for the first time in a long time.

Then he turned and walked into the fog.

Because somewhere, in some office, someone was already building the next machine.

And he intended to be there when the first gear turned.

Chapter 25
The Clean Man's War

Spring 1874 – New York City

John Kelly didn't need a gang of thieves.

He didn't need backroom cigar deals or courthouse vaults lined with kickbacks.

He didn't roar.

He purged.

After Tweed's fall, Kelly rose from the ashes like a bishop in full vestment, clean hands, clean books, clean conscience. A pious Catholic, former congressman and former sheriff of the city, he wore virtue like armor and carried his rosary in one hand while consolidating power with the other.

To the public he was the answer.

To Crowley he was a scalpel in a world of axes.

The change was immediate. Courts quieted. The press calmed. The Committee of Seventy disbanded with a final report and a handshake. Contractors began winning bids again, this time with the proper paperwork and the proper smiles.

And yet the grift never stopped.

It evolved.

Crowley saw it first in zoning records. Entire blocks were quietly reclassified and resold between shell corporations and Catholic charities. Roads that existed only on paper were paved and repaved, twice, sometimes three times, by firms with no offices and no employees.

The same machine.

Now with polish.

Then the message came. An envelope, no return address. Inside: a formal invitation to a retirement dinner for a judge Crowley had never met. His name misspelled as "D. Crowlie." A mistake. Not a coincidence. That was how Kelly played. He let you know when he'd turned his eyes toward you, politely, subtly, like a man setting down a scalpel just before the incision.

Then George Bliss Jr. was attacked.

A brick through the carriage window. Brass knuckles across his jaw. No theft. No robbery. Just a warning. He spent three days in Bellevue, jaw wired, unable to speak.

When Crowley visited, Bliss scribbled on a pad:

"They're not trying to kill me. Just bury the case."

Then came Delaney, a clerk in the city deed office who'd slipped Crowley forged property titles tied to a Brooklyn bishop and a known Tammany front. He never made it to the follow-up meeting. They found him in a dry well on Staten Island. Hands broken. Ledger gone.

The war had changed. There were no press leaks. No angry juries. No bold headlines. It was a cold war in shadows, one that consumed men silently and erased their footprints.

Crowley adapted.

He stopped working from precincts. He worked from basements, dry-goods stalls, candle-lit rooms above Irish boarding houses. He wrote in invisible ink. He backed up every name, every deed, every fraudulent street paving into coded duplicates and spread them across the city like seeds in dry earth.

Then he began recruiting. Not reformers, survivors. An ex-cop thrown off the force for refusing to frame a rival. A civil clerk with a morphine habit and a grudge against a judge. A drunken alderman who once wrote speeches for Tweed and now lived off boiled potatoes and regret.

They weren't saints. They weren't bought either. They became the spine of Crowley's own machine, not to steal, but to expose. Not to climb. To collapse.

He sent faked letters between phantom companies to test whether they would show in tax records. They did. He mapped 113 public-works payments to addresses that turned out to be abandoned tenements or nonexistent storefronts. Paved roads to ghost neighborhoods. Bridges to nowhere.

He didn't just investigate anymore. He documented collapse.

The night they unveiled a statue to John Kelly in Tompkins Square, crowds roared with pride. Irish laborers cheered. Priests blessed it. The Times ran the headline: "From Shame to Saint: Kelly's Moral Machine."

Crowley stood across the street, collar turned up, pistol holstered but loaded, not to fire, to witness. To see the face of the man who had gutted Tweed's crimes and dressed them in robes.

He didn't want justice anymore.

He wanted annihilation.

And he knew now, Kelly's machine wouldn't fall with indictments or courtrooms.

It would fall in fire.

He was ready to strike the match.

Chapter 26
Family in the Shadows

New York City, 1873–1884

The city never slept. But sometimes, if you stood still long enough, it pretended to.

In those quiet hours between streetlamp flickers and the clatter of milk carts, David Crowley sat in his apartment on 144th Street, staring out at the soot-streaked brick across the alley, holding the silence like fragile glass.

It wasn't just the fight that kept him alive anymore.

It was David Jr.

Born January 13, 1873, his name was more than legacy, it was resolve. The boy had his father's stubborn eyes and his mother's kindness. From the moment the nurse placed him in Crowley's arms, everything changed. The fire he had once aimed at Tammany now burned for something smaller, fiercer: protection. He would carve a future from this city, even if he had to bleed for every brick.

Mary Agnes watched her husband soften around their son. She never mentioned the bruises on his knuckles when he came home late, or the fresh ink stains from hidden ledgers. She only asked, "Is he safe?"

And David always said yes.

Even when he wasn't sure.

Two years later, on May 12, 1875, Mary was born.

She came into the world under gray skies and low thunder, but cried with the lungs of a storm. Crowley stood outside the birthing room again, fists clenched, praying without words.

When the midwife handed him the swaddled child, his breath caught. She had his jaw but her mother's calm, soft, patient, steady.

And still, the city moved.

In October 1877 came Lillian Teresa, red hair, quick wit, and eyes that seemed to know too much. By her third birthday she had memorized every vendor's name on the block.

If David Jr. gave Crowley hope, and Mary gave him peace, then Lillian gave him warning: the world would not wait. You had to chase it or be swallowed whole.

Their apartment above the grocer was narrow, hot in summer and freezing in winter, but it breathed with life.

Mary Agnes ruled it gently, cooking stews from scraps, humming Irish hymns, lining windows with lavender and prayer cards. She kept the girls dressed, the boy polished, and her husband grounded. She never demanded less of him, only reminded him what he stood to lose.

In the evenings, the shadows thinned.

David Jr. read aloud from the Catholic Herald.

Mary climbed into her father's lap and traced the scars on his wrist with tiny fingers.

Lillian lectured her stuffed rabbit about voter fraud, mimicking her father's tone with eerie precision.

But even as warmth grew inside their home, death waited outside.

In the spring of 1880, it came for David Jr.

A fever, sudden and merciless. By the time the doctor arrived, his pulse was too faint.

Crowley held his boy's hand until it stilled, whispering stories of soldiers and bravery that the child would never live to become.

Six months later, it came for Mary -(The baby)

A coughing sickness that worsened with each dusk. Crowley bought every cure peddled on the street. None of them worked. She died in their bed, her hand still wrapped around his, a rosary pressed between them. He buried her next to David Jr. in Calvary Cemetery.

For a time, silence ruled the apartment.

Even Lillian stopped asking questions.

But the city did not stop.

In July 1884, Crowley returned from a courthouse errand to find a midwife waiting in the hall.

The baby had come early, another boy.

Mary Agnes had named him George.

Crowley added the middle name himself: Bliss.

George Bliss Crowley.

A tribute. A promise. A message to the man who had never stopped believing in him.

Lillian, now seven, took to her brother with surprising calm. She rocked him, sang to him, told him secrets she wouldn't share with adults. And for Crowley, it was the closest thing to salvation he would ever know, a daughter with fire, a son with purpose, a home rebuilt from ash.

But he never let go of the fight.

The ledgers stayed hidden beneath the floorboards.

Names etched in invisible ink.

Secrets tucked inside holy books.

Mary was gone.

David Jr. was gone.

But George breathed.

And for that, Crowley sharpened his knives.

Because the war wasn't over.

It had just learned how to knock softly.

Chapter 27
The Slow Burn

New York City, 1874

Tweed was gone.

But the rot remained.

His downfall made headlines, cartoons of him in chains, sermons proclaiming a reborn New York, reformers shouting in the streets about a city finally cleansed.

But in the neighborhoods where tenements leaned against each other like drunks, nothing really changed.

The candles still sputtered out in Five Points.

The priests still preached loyalty from pulpits thick with incense.

And in the courthouses, the same clerks and bailiffs, men who had stamped Tweed's fraud yesterday, were stamping seals for the next buyer today.

Into that silence stepped John Kelly.

He didn't thunder like Tweed. He didn't boast or swagger.

Kelly's genius was in quiet erosion.

He didn't buy power.

He dissolved into it.

Judges were no longer bribed, they married into families of influence.

Priests were not threatened, they were funded to feed the poor.

Kelly handed out bread, coal, and jobs, and asked for nothing in return, at least, not visibly.

The papers praised him.

"The Good Boss."

A new era. A steady hand after Tweed's corruption.

Crowley wasn't fooled.

He saw the shift from his post in the precinct, watching Kelly's lieutenants move through the city like undertakers in silk gloves.

They didn't shout. They whispered.

They didn't steal elections. They made people give them away out of gratitude.

Bullets couldn't touch a man like Kelly.

Indictments wouldn't stick.

Witnesses either vanished, or turned.

So Crowley chose a different weapon.

Phase One: The Records

It began with scraps.

Court dockets copied by hand before clerks "lost" the originals.

Deeds and tax receipts smuggled from dusty offices by young assistants he paid in nickels and promises.

Photographs of land sales snapped by archivists moments before Tammany seals made them disappear.

He bribed auctioneers, failing notaries, and parish bookkeepers too broke, or too frightened, to stay loyal.

And slowly, methodically, he **built**.

One book for deeds.

One for zoning.

One for church-run charities claiming false tax exemptions.

The numbers turned his stomach.

Between 1877 and 1882, over forty percent of road repairs were duplicated, some triplicated.

Entire sewer lines billed on paper but never dug in the ground.

By candlelight, in a cramped tenement room, he mapped it all.

Each street. Each lot. Each name.

When the first ledger was complete, he realized what he held.

Not a case.

Not evidence for trial.

But a weapon, heavy, silent, patient.

A book that could outlast Kelly's power, if he lived long enough to use it.

That night, Crowley bound it in twine and sealed it behind a false wall.

He didn't pray.

He didn't drink.

He just sat in the dark, watching the shadows flicker, knowing the war had changed.

It wasn't about indictments anymore.

It was about outliving the machine.

And somewhere, in the dim light of a saloon near the Battery, a new player was already rising.

Richard Croker.

He didn't look like a boss. He looked like a boxer.

Because he had been one.

A former prizefighter turned alderman, Croker had broad shoulders, fists like stone, and a jaw that had absorbed more punches than truths. But beneath the brute frame was something colder, a mind sharpened by street politics and backroom deals.

He watched Kelly from the corner of every meeting.

Never interrupting.

Never challenging.

Always nodding.

He wore black to funerals.

Never smiled in public.

And when he spoke, he made words sound like contracts.

He was patient.

He was precise.

He was the next storm.

One night in 1874, Kelly slid a folded letter across a table to a senior ward boss.

Crowley wouldn't see that letter until years later, smuggled out by a clerk whose brother had been jailed on a ghost warrant.

On the back, in a clipped, slanted hand, it read:

"When the weight shifts, he takes the wheel."

, Croker

Crowley didn't know it then.

But the next chapter of the war had already begun.

The man who would bury Tammany's last pretense of virtue was already waiting in the wings, silent, coiled, and ready.

The fight was no longer about who ruled.

It was about who was still standing when the smoke cleared.

Chapter 28
The Gravediggers

New York City, 1878

He didn't hire reformers.

Reformers wanted speeches, headlines, purity.

Reformers got themselves killed.

Crowley hired the broken.

They were called many things, informants, snitches, burnouts.

But Crowley called them the Gravediggers.

Not because they buried bodies, but because they dug up what the city tried hardest to hide: its own paper trail.

The first was Henry Malloy, a failed auctioneer with a whiskey cough who had once moved fake lumber for Tammany. Bankrupt, blacklisted, sleeping in a Chinatown boarding house, Malloy still remembered the codes, the signatures, the middlemen. His memory was worth more than gold.

The second was Sister Agnes.

No longer a sister, excommunicated for forging baptismal records in the Five Corners orphan scheme. She knew the handwriting of priests who had signed off on false adoptions. She could spot a counterfeit seal at twenty paces.

The third was Thomas Burke, a schoolteacher dismissed for accusing a ward boss of embezzling textbook funds. He'd lost his post, his pension, and his reputation, but not his bitterness. He could recite budgets by year, tell you which schools got desks and which got lies.

Each came to Crowley not out of loyalty, but out of need, hunger, desperation, revenge.

He taught them to code records, to write in ledgers that read like riddles to anyone but them.

He had them scatter duplicates across the city:

- One ledger hidden inside a hollowed hymnal.
- Another slipped beneath a floorboard in a Bowery bookshop.
- A third rolled tight into a drainpipe behind Mulberry Street.

Nothing was ever in one place.

If Kelly burned a building, six more bled proof.

Their work was quiet, endless, and dangerous.

They met in alleyways, abandoned lofts, shuttered taverns.

They whispered more than they spoke.

They carried no banners, no titles.

Crowley watched them one evening in the flicker of a gas lamp, each hunched over a desk, scratching ink onto paper.

Broken people, all of them.

Yet here they were, crafting a weapon stronger than pistols or clubs.

Outside, Kelly's men were handing out coal to widows and blankets to orphans.

The newspapers sang his praises.

The Good Boss.

The People's Protector.

Crowley turned from the window, the ledger heavy in his hands.

"Saviors don't need ledgers," he muttered.

"Tyrants do."

And in that moment, he understood.

He was no longer fighting a man.

He was fighting memory itself, the kind Kelly bought, erased, or buried.

The Gravediggers would make sure some memories survived.

Chapter 29
Containment

New York City, 1880

Crowley knew better than to swing for Kelly's head. You don't fight a fortress by charging its gates. You chip at its foundations, quietly, patiently.

That was **Phase Two**: Containment.

He began with whispers. Anonymous letters slipped beneath church doors, unsigned pamphlets seeded in parish halls. They never named Kelly outright. They spoke instead of "discrepancies" in parish funds, of donations that vanished between collection plates and widows' tables, of streets paved twice but never once inspected.

Then came the soup kitchens. Not city-sponsored, not church-run. Just tables set up on Kelly's turf, Mulberry, Catherine, Baxter, serving stew and bread to whoever came. Paid for by donations from men and women Tammany had ruined: a bankrupt printer, a widow overcharged on rent by a ward boss, a shopkeeper fined out of business. They funded the meals in silence, and Crowley made sure no name was attached.

At first, Kelly's men laughed. Charity without credit? Food without speeches? It was nothing.

But when the lines for soup stretched longer than the lines at Kelly's coal depots, the laughter stopped.

Crowley printed pamphlets next, The Committee for Municipal Fairness. They looked official, neutral. Inside, they were packed with facts: fraudulent contracts, ghost payrolls, false deeds. Every word verifiable. Every line a blade.

No one knew the author, but the information was impossible to ignore.

The murmurs began in the streets of Five Points. Not shouts, murmurs.

A ward boss who pocketed half a widow's pension.

A paving company billing for streets that didn't exist.

A priest blessing an orphanage that had no orphans.

Kelly noticed.

By 1884, the new police commissioner, his own man, was forced to investigate ghost payrolls. Three names surfaced, all real, all tied back to contracts Kelly had signed. The press gave it two inches on the third page, but inside City Hall, the tremor was felt.

Kelly adjusted. He no longer held meetings in council chambers, where minutes might be kept. Instead, he chose church basements and rented tavern back rooms. He changed his driver, altered his routes, whispered orders through priests instead of aldermen.

He began to look over his shoulder.

So did Crowley.

For every ledger he compiled, for every proof he duplicated, there were eyes in the street. He couldn't tell which coal man or street sweeper had been bought. He walked home differently each night, never the same route twice.

One evening, as he crossed Mulberry Street, he glimpsed a man in a bowler hat watching him from a lamppost. When Crowley turned, the man was gone.

That night, he placed a duplicate of his largest ledger in a sealed tin box beneath the floorboards of a Bowery print shop. Only the Gravediggers knew where it was.

The war was invisible. Exhausting. Slow.

Kelly still looked untouchable, his name sung from pulpits, his generosity painted in newsprint.

But Crowley felt the shiver in the air, the first fracture in Kelly's armor.

The city wasn't shouting.

Not yet.

But it was murmuring.

And murmurs had toppled giants before.

Chapter 30
The Ledger and the Turning Point

New York City, 1883

By now the ledger was the size of a tombstone.

Years of ink and sweat, carried in hidden satchels, stashed in false walls, copied twice, sometimes three times. Each page a scar in paper. Every name, every contract, every false seal lived inside Crowley's books. If they ever saw daylight, they would not merely bruise Kelly's empire. They would eviscerate it.

One page stood out above the rest.

A triangular transaction, elegant in its brazenness:

- A Catholic orphanage in Brooklyn that supposedly cared for one hundred and forty children.
- A Manhattan paving company billing for repairs to streets that did not exist.
- A judge's widow who had "purchased" five East River lots from the city at one-eighth their value.

The signatures matched. The dates aligned. The deed was real. But the authorization had been forged, the ink traced by a clerk paid too well to ask questions.

Crowley didn't merely have the documents. He had something rarer: a witness.

Seamus Daly had once been a bookkeeper, crippled now, hunched, dragging one leg. He'd worked in Kelly's orbit for years, keeping ledgers for a contractor who serviced both the paving company and the orphanage. He had watched the same numbers repeat, the same lots sold, the same money laundered through false charities. In a moment of regret, or maybe cowardice, he had copied it all into a duplicate ledger.

"For confession someday," Daly had rasped, voice like broken glass.

That day had come.

Crowley laid the fourteen documents on the café table: two forged authorizations, a chain of deeds, one affidavit signed by Daly himself. The evidence was not mere corruption. It was rot that ran from City Hall to the chancery.

This was not about a crooked alderman or a barroom bribe. This was about Kelly's last veil of virtue, the Church.

Later that fall, Café behind the Courthouse

George Bliss was older now. He carried the weight of years; the fight was still in his eyes but slower in his step. The once-fiery prosecutor had traded the courtroom for quiet consulting, but Crowley trusted him more than anyone.

They met in a narrow café tucked behind the courthouse, the kind of place where clerks took whiskey in the afternoons and no one asked questions.

Crowley slid the file across the table. Fourteen documents. Two ledgers. One sworn affidavit. The wood creaked beneath the weight.

Bliss studied the stack, flipping each page with deliberate care. He paused on the orphanage ledger, frowned at the forged authorization, then looked up.

"This does not take down a precinct," Bliss said quietly. "This takes down the Church, the courts, and Kelly's last veil of virtue."

Crowley leaned back; the lamp threw half his face into shadow. "That's the point."

Bliss tapped the table, the sound a small, judicial knock. "You ready to go public?"

Crowley's eyes were steady. "No. I'm ready to burn it all."

The words hung between them. A trolley clanged past outside. Inside, only the scrape of chair legs filled the silence.

Bliss closed the folder and slid it back. "You understand, David. If you move on this, if you even leak the shape of it, Kelly will not come for your papers. He will come for you. He will burn your name before he ever burns your ledgers."

Crowley nodded. He had accepted that risk the night he wrote the first casebook. This was never about living clean. It was about leaving something behind that could not be erased.

"Then let him try," he said. "Because if he burns me, this ledger burns him."

That night

Crowley walked home through streets washed in gaslight and fog. His boots clicked on cobbles slick with rain. Somewhere in the dark he thought he heard footsteps trailing his own, steady, patient. He turned once and saw nothing.

When he reached his building he did not climb to his room immediately. He pulled the ledger tight against his chest, feeling its weight, and thought of the names inside: priests, widows, judges, aldermen. Every one a nail in Kelly's coffin.

But coffins went both ways. Crowley, more than anyone, knew the city kept two kinds of ledgers: the ones you wrote, and the one written about you.

It was only a matter of time before someone began filling his.

Chapter 31
Fire on Madison Street

December 13, 1883, Lower East Side, New York City

The city was still half-asleep when the fire broke loose.

204 Madison Street was just another tenement, leaning brick, broken shutters, a rat's nest of families packed so tight the walls sweated in summer. By dawn, it was a furnace.

Crowley saw the glow as he turned the corner on his way to the Seventh Precinct. At first he thought it was lamplight caught in fog. Then the smoke rose, thick, black, rolling upward as if the sky itself were burning.

The screams confirmed it.

He ran. His boots struck cobblestones slick with frost, lungs burning colder than the air. A crowd had gathered but kept their distance, faces pale in the fire's glow. Women clutched shawls to their mouths, men pulled caps low, but none moved toward the door.

The heat hit like a slap, the doorway already vomiting flame. Inside, timbers cracked like rifles.

Then, above the roar, a woman's shriek, thin and ragged. Followed by smaller, panicked cries of children.

He didn't think. He never did in moments like this. Instinct carried him, the same instinct that had carried him through Gettysburg, through the Fenian alleys, through Kelly's slow suffocation of the city.

He tore off his coat, pulled it across his mouth, and plunged inside.

The smoke was blinding, thick as wool. Every breath clawed his chest raw. He climbed the stairs by touch, one hand on the rail, the other reaching forward into darkness. The building groaned, ready to collapse beneath him.

On the second floor he found them, Margaret Sahlen, clutching her two daughters. Both girls crying into her skirts. Her face gray with soot, eyes wide with terror.

"Help us!" she rasped.

He moved fast. He wrapped the smaller girl in his coat, scooped the older under his arm, and seized Margaret by the wrist. Together they staggered down the stairwell, boards breaking beneath their feet, heat chasing them like a predator.

A neighbor's hand shot through the smoke, then they were out, coughing, stumbling, collapsing into the cold December air.

The crowd surged. Cheers. Gasps. Margaret sobbing as she clutched her children, unwilling to let go.

"You saved us," she whispered, eyes streaming.

Crowley nodded once, already turning away. Because even as the crowd pressed forward, even as the night rang with gratitude, his instincts whispered something darker. He could feel eyes in the crowd, lingering not with admiration but with calculation.

He had made himself visible. And visibility was dangerous.

December 18, 1883 , Seventh Precinct

The room smelled of polish and pipe smoke. Brass buttons gleamed; medals caught the gaslight. Reporters lined the back wall, notebooks ready.

"Sergeant David Crowley," the Commissioner announced, pinning the medal of merit to his chest, "for uncommon bravery in the service of this city."

Applause filled the hall. Officers clapped dutifully, a few with genuine warmth. Margaret Sahlen stood near the front, tears bright on her cheeks, her children clutching her skirts.

Crowley bowed his head, shook the Commissioner's hand, accepted the medal. But his eyes weren't on the brass.

They were on the reporters.

He knew how this city worked. One week's hero became next week's scandal. A medal was just another piece of leverage, another excuse for scrutiny. And he had more to hide than most, ledgers heavy with proof, files tucked in drainpipes and hymnals, confessions waiting for daylight.

Bliss's warning echoed in his head: If you move on Kelly, he won't just come for your papers. He'll come for you.

Crowley adjusted the medal, the ribbon already cold. The applause washed over him, hollow as church bells in an empty parish.

He felt the trap tightening.

Somewhere behind those reporters' pencils, the first whispers were already being shaped. Names like Margaret Sahlen and Maggie Morris would mix, blur, twist. His rescue would fade. Another story would take its place.

Today's hero. Tomorrow's suspect.

And in New York, the city never let you choose which ledger you ended up in.

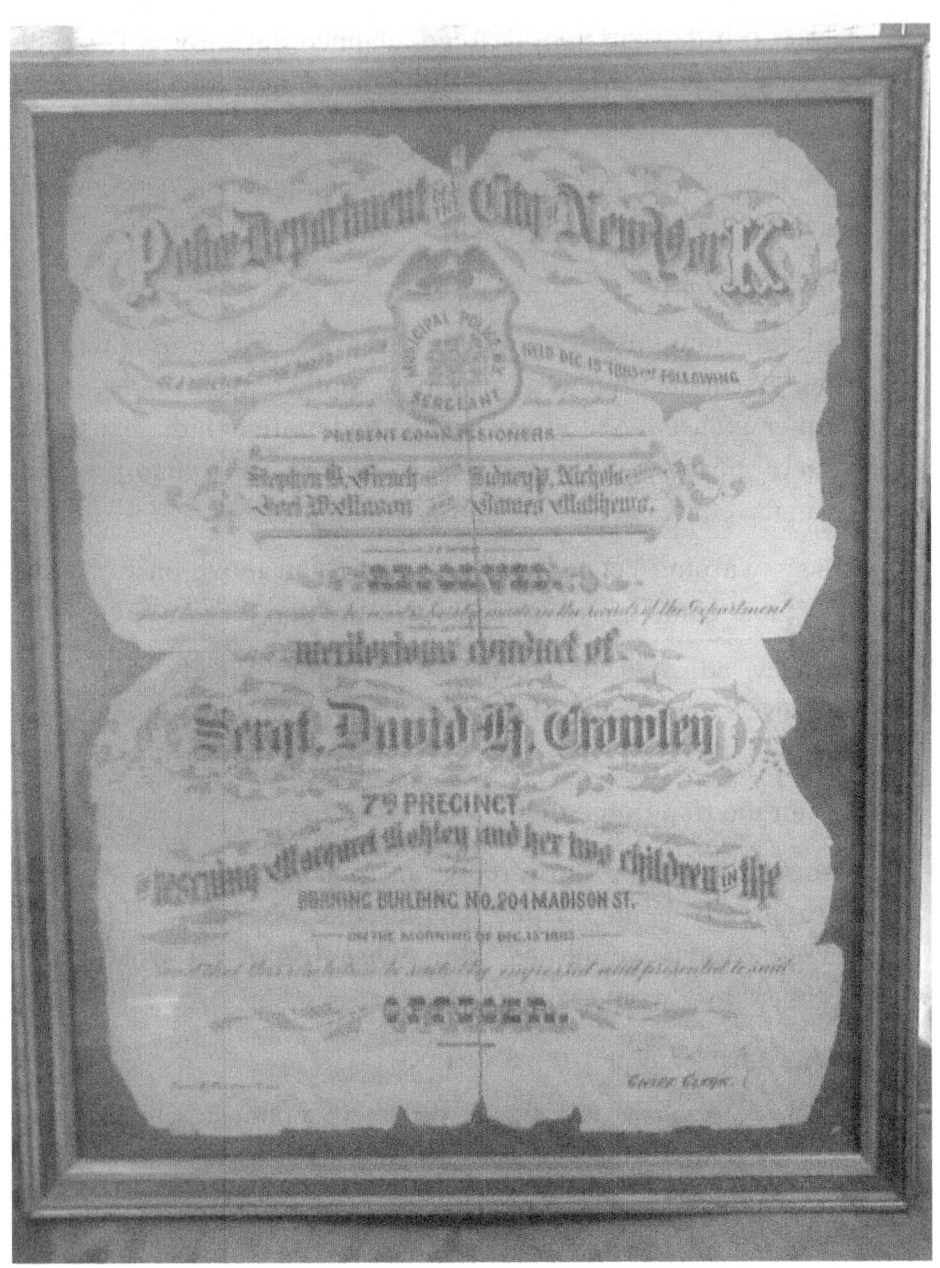

Chapter 32
The Watchers

New York City, Early 1884

The fire medal still hung in his wardrobe, bright against the dark wool of his uniform. He rarely wore it now. Crowley knew better than to flaunt anything the city gave you, it always found a way to take it back.

But the medal wasn't the only thing that lingered. Since the rescue on Madison Street, he had felt eyes on him. Not always, not in ways he could prove, just enough to raise the hair on the back of his neck.

A man in a bowler hat loitered across from the Seventh Precinct three mornings in a row. Gone by the time Crowley crossed the street. A carriage sat too long outside his building, its curtains drawn, wheels turning slow, as if its driver had no destination. Twice, he spotted the same parish priest at corners miles apart, watching with a face too carefully blank.

The city was full of watchers. But these ones were patient. They weren't thieves or thugs. They were surveyors, charting the terrain before a strike.

Margaret Sahlen came to see him in February, her two girls in tow, both clutching his hands as though he were family. They'd baked him bread, coarse and uneven, but warm and honest.

"You saved us," she said again, eyes filling as though the fire had been yesterday. "I wanted them to remember your face."

Crowley smiled gently, knelt to the children, accepted the bread. But when he walked them out, he caught sight of the bowler hat again, just beyond the corner. Watching. Always watching.

The Gravediggers were feeling it too.

Henry Malloy, the ruined auctioneer, arrived at their meeting with one eye swollen shut. He said he'd stumbled. Crowley didn't press. Sister Agnes confessed she'd been followed for three blocks by men she swore were Kelly's, their silence louder than any threat. A week later, Thomas Burke didn't show at all. His boarding house room was empty, bed unslept in. No one ever saw him again.

Crowley's ledgers were safe, for now. Hidden in drainpipes, pews, hollowed books. But safety was relative. Kelly didn't need to burn the books to kill their power. He only needed to kill the man who wrote them.

Bliss met him for whiskey one rain-slick night behind the courthouse. The old prosecutor studied him with the same sharp gaze that once cut through perjured testimony.

"You're too visible," Bliss said flatly. "You rescue a woman and her children, they give you a medal, and now half the city knows your name. That was never your game, David. You were a shadow man. Invisible. Kelly doesn't strike shadows. He strikes what he can see."

Crowley drained his glass and set it down slow. "So what do I do? Hide?"

Bliss shook his head. "No. You prepare. Because the strike is coming. Not with bullets, Kelly's too careful for that. He'll wait, he'll study, and when the city's ready, he'll pick the one story that can burn you."

Crowley stared at the rain beating the window, unease tightening in his gut. He knew Bliss was right. Kelly's watchers weren't scouting targets. They were scouting weaknesses.

And in New York, weakness always had a name.

Chapter 33
Ashes and Ink

New York City, Autumn 1884

The fire began just before dawn, when the streets were still empty and the milk carts had not yet rolled from the stables. A municipal records office in Brooklyn, one of three that held tax deeds, street contracts, and zoning ledgers, went up like kindling.

By the time Crowley arrived, summoned by a whisper from one of his clerks, the building was ash. The walls sagged, black and skeletal, smoke still bleeding from the ruins. A dozen clerks stood shivering in the street, faces gray with shock.

The official report called it an accident, a faulty stove, poor wiring. But Crowley knew better. He smelled kerosene in the rubble. He saw how certain cabinets had been pried open before the fire ever reached them.

It wasn't a fire. It was a message.

That night, in a shuttered boarding house off Canal Street, he gathered what was left of the Gravediggers. Sister Agnes paced, her rosary beads clattering in restless fingers. Malloy sat hunched, coughing into a handkerchief, his eyes raw from smoke or fear, it was hard to tell.

"They're burning the trail," Crowley said, laying a charred scrap of paper on the table. "And they knew exactly which files to hit."

"Then they know about us," Malloy rasped.

"They know someone is copying," Crowley corrected. "They don't know where it all is. Yet."

He saw it in their faces, the fear. They weren't soldiers. They were citizens hollowed by loss, each carrying a reason to hate the machine and yet too fragile to face its teeth. Kelly's fire had done more than burn records; it had burned resolve.

Crowley leaned forward, voice low and measured. "That's why we scatter. No single point of failure. No one person holding the key." He slid parcels across the table, each one wrapped in oilskin. "Pieces of the ledger. Hide them, a pew, a drainpipe, a printshop drawer. Spread them. If they burn one, five more survive."

The Gravediggers nodded, though the weight of the task showed in their eyes.

Later that week, Bliss poured him a whiskey in a quiet corner of a tavern. The old prosecutor's face was more lined, his eyes harder than ever.

"This is escalation," Bliss said. "You're forcing Kelly to fight in daylight. He doesn't like it."

Crowley shook his head. "No. He's probing. Testing. He doesn't need to burn my ledgers to beat me. He only has to burn my name."

Bliss studied him for a long moment, then said softly, "And that's exactly what he'll do."

That night, Crowley returned to his tenement. He lit a lamp, unrolled one of his duplicate ledgers, and read by the flickering light. Pages of names, contracts, ghost payrolls, false deeds, it was all there, enough to choke a courthouse.

But as he turned the pages, he noticed the ink stains on his hands, dark smudges that wouldn't wash out. He stared at them in the lamplight, the smell of smoke still clinging to him from Brooklyn's ruins.

Ashes and ink. That was all the city ever left behind.

And sooner or later, he feared, it would leave nothing of him but the same.

Chapter 34
The Winter Ledger

New York City, Winter 1884–1885

Snow fell in slow, stubborn flakes that turned to gray paste by morning. The city moved through it anyway, hunched, impatient, unrepentant. Crowley watched from his window on 144th Street, sleeve rolled to the elbow, ink drying on his knuckles like a confession he couldn't wash away.

He should have been sleeping. Instead, he waited on a knock.

It came just before midnight, three soft raps, a pause, then two. The Gravediggers' signal.

Sister Agnes slipped inside with the cold. She kept the hood of her shawl up and her eyes down, the old habit of hiding in plain sight.

"You walked?" Crowley asked.

"Carriages are noticed," she said. "Sinners aren't."

She set a parcel on the table, oilskin, tightly bound. Crowley cut the twine with his pocketknife and drew the papers into the lamplight.

Not just papers. A vein straight into Kelly's heart.

First: a baptismal register from a Brooklyn parish, entries rewritten, names doubled, dates shifted forward, then back again. Each change matched a transfer from the parish orphans fund into a trust account that belonged to no parish at all.

Second: the trust deed, innocent on its face, routing those funds to a shell company that bought five East River lots at one-eighth value. The signature belonged to a judge's widow. The authorization was a forgery.

Third: a payroll list from City Works, six men paid for paving streets that didn't exist, each "witnessed" by a foreman whose name appeared in two places at once.

And tucked among them, smaller, humbler than the rest, a notarized letter in a cramped, careful hand:

I kept a second book because I feared God more than Kelly. , Seamus Daly

Crowley didn't sit. He read standing, the way a man hears his own sentence.

Agnes folded her arms to steady her hands. "The chancery clerk who let me see the register, he's gone. They say he took a job in Albany. He didn't pack a trunk."

Crowley nodded once. "Then we move faster."

"You mean louder."

"I mean safer." He slid the register toward her. "We split the vein. Three copies. Three paths. If they burn one, two still bleed."

Agnes glanced at the bedroom door. "And your family?"

He followed her eyes.

Mary Agnes stirred in her sleep, a hand on the cradle where infant George breathed in tiny, earnest pulls. Lillian's curls spilled across a small pillow at the foot of the bed, an arm flung wide, a child claiming space in a world that never gave enough.

"They're the reason this ledger lives," he said softly. "Not the risk."

Agnes exhaled, the sound a small prayer with no amen. "I'll take the parish book tonight. Hymnals shift on Sundays. So do sins."

She left as she'd come, quiet, the door catching only once before it closed.

Two days later, the city struck back, never with a headline, always with a rumor.

Henry Malloy arrived to their meeting late and wrong. Someone had put a warning in his face, the kind that fades to a color you wear for a week. He said he'd slipped on ice. Crowley didn't ask where ice learned to clench a fist.

They worked by candle until the stubs burned out, parceling pages, coding margins, assigning drops: a drainpipe in Mulberry Alley, a pew hinge at St. Brigid's, a false bottom in a Bowery print drawer nobody rented anymore.

When the last envelope was sealed, Malloy lingered at the door, hat in hand. "You ever think about ending it?" he asked. "Not surrender. Just, stop pulling the tail of the beast."

Crowley looked at his hands, blacked with ink, and thought of kerosene soaking a municipal office. "Every day," he said. "Then I remember who writes the ending if I don't."

Malloy nodded, satisfied or simply out of questions, and disappeared into the snow.

Bliss poured whiskey with the precision of a man who had measured other men's lives by the ounce. They sat in a booth behind the courthouse where the wood remembered a thousand sworn lies.

"You have enough to wake the dead," Bliss said, turning one page at a time as if each had weight. "Or at least to make them talk."

"Then we speak first," Crowley said.

Bliss didn't look up. "Public?"

"No." Crowley tapped the ledger's spine. "Insurance. A package, copies and a letter. If I disappear, or they hang something ugly on me, this lands on the Times editor's desk, the Methodist Council, and the state's attorney in Albany on the same morning."

Bliss closed the book. "You're planning for your own obituary."

"I'm planning for theirs."

Silence held the table. Outside, a trolley bell cut the night.

Bliss set both hands flat on the wood. "He won't shoot you, David. That would make you a martyr. He'll poison the well. He'll turn your name to mud, and once it is, no court will drink from your ledger."

Crowley thought of the cradle, the small blanket, the medal that slept in the wardrobe where he refused to wear it. "Then I write faster than he lies."

Bliss gave half a smile that had nothing to do with humor. "I've seen men outpace bullets. I've never seen one outrun a rumor."

February sharpened to glass. The city's breath froze on its own teeth. Crowley walked alternate routes home, counting the watchers without letting them know they'd been counted, the bowler hat at Catherine Street, the priest whose collar changed parish by parish, the carriage that never seemed to have a driver's face.

The city was patient.

The city was watching.

And somewhere behind its shutters, Kelly, or someone younger, hungrier, was already writing his version of the ledger.

Chapter 35
The Bait

Spring 1885 | New York City

It was never about guilt.

It was about removal.

By 1885, David Crowley had become more than a nuisance to Tammany. He was a structural threat, an investigator turned insurgent, undermining the foundations of the machine itself. His reports, quietly circulated among reformers, clerks, and backchannels, threatened to expose land fraud, clergy kickbacks, and entire wards of ghost infrastructure.

He had no office. No badge. Just truth, and a growing army of believers.

John Kelly didn't rage. He didn't threaten.

He sanctioned.

And the men at the long velvet table in the Tammany Club knew what that meant.

They chose **Maggie Morris.**

Not because she was willing, because she was pliable.

She had debts. A mother in a Bowery infirmary. A brother in the Tombs. The Hall offered her a clean slate, a white dress, and enough money to vanish afterward.

They told her a story. Fed her a lie.

"Crowley is dangerous. He's hurting the people. You're helping protect others."

She believed them, at first.

By the time she doubted, it was too late.

Standard Hall, East Broadway , The Benefit Dance

A hired band. Paper lanterns. Enough whiskey to keep the air wet.

The "charity" was legitimate on paper, but the real work was below.

Crowley entered just past ten.

He wasn't there to dance. Never was.

He was following a lead, a name: **Burns**, tied to sewer grading fraud. A man who existed only in whispers and false ledgers.

He scanned the crowd. Bartenders. Doormen. Nothing familiar.

Then she appeared.

Maggie dropped a glove. Her voice was warm, a little too eager.

She said she knew his name. Knew of his work.

"My uncle said you helped the widows on Third Street. You stood up to the city board."

Crowley blinked. Hesitated.

A small compliment. One thread of sincerity.

And that's how they caught him.

They talked for six minutes.

No drinks. No touches. No lowering of defenses.

She asked about his work. He deflected.

She said she wanted to help. He told her to forget his name.

She asked if he'd walk her downstairs, "just for a breath."

He did.

He never entered the room.

He stood in the doorway, looked, said something about the air being too heavy. Then turned and walked back up the stairs.

Maggie didn't follow.

She waited.

Then she screamed.

By the time the first constable arrived, she was sobbing in the arms of a matron.

Ten minutes later, she gave the name: **David Crowley.**

By dawn, Justice Duffy had signed the arrest warrant.

The Arrest

Superintendent Walling sent Sergeant **Cahill**, one of Kelly's own, to Madison Avenue.

Crowley had barely slept. He answered the door in the same coat he'd worn to Standard Hall. Shirt unbuttoned. Holster empty. Still half in the fog of disbelief.

The cuffs were already out.

"Is this a mistake?" he asked.

Cahill said nothing.

"This is Hedden and Leary," Crowley muttered. "Tell them I'll get square."

The street was quiet. Two carriages passed. His son watched from the stairs.

No crowd. No protest.

Just a man being erased.

The Papers

By the 8:00 edition, it was everywhere:

SERGEANT ARRESTED FOR ATTACK AT EAST BROADWAY BALL

YOUNG SHOPGIRL TELLS OF HORROR IN LOCKED ROOM

CROWLEY, LONG A CRITIC OF CITY GOVERNMENT, ACCUSED IN SHOCKING ASSAULT

They ran Maggie's statement in full.

Not his.

They printed every blemish from his service file, the pistol incident on Worth Street, the insubordination charge from '77.

Not a word about the commendations.

Not a word about the war.

The editors didn't write it as fact.

They wrote it as inevitability.

The New York Herald:

Saturday evening, in company with several friends, she attended a ball held in Standard Hall, No. 165 East Broadway. It was a benefit tendered to Frank B. Le Maire, of No. 239 Henry-street.

The complainant says that Sergt. Crowley entered the hall about 2 o'clock yesterday morning. He was in an intoxicated condition. Miss Morris was introduced to the new arrival by a young man named Burns. Crowley, she says, made himself very "sociable," and asked her to have some refreshments. She refused, but he insisted, and he took her arm and led her to the bar room on the floor below where the dancing was going on. It was locked, but the bartender, William Blint, of No. 1 Essex-street, was found. He opened the door and offered to serve the drinks. Crowley ordered some whisky for himself and sarsaparilla for his companion. When the drinks were brought the girl said she thought her sarsaparilla smelled strongly of liquor. To satisfy herself, however, she tasted it and convinced herself that there was some whisky or some other strong liquor in her drink. She refused to take any of it, saying, "I don't feel dry."

The bartender, the girl said, at this point left the room and locked the door. Crowley then began to act in an insulting manner. "He showed me his pistol," she said, "and intimated that if I made any noise or outcry he would shoot me. Then he threw me on a billiard table and assaulted me."

Several of the friends of the girl were alarmed at her prolonged absence, and they went down stairs to the bar room. There they found the bartender on guard, and he refused to allow anybody to pass in. One of the girls who came down stairs, Celia Joyce, of No. 31 Monroe-street, made an outcry and demanded admittance. The noise attracted the attention of Roundsman Walsh, of the Seventh Precinct, who was passing the door at the time. He went in and compelled the bartender to open the door. On going inside he found Miss Morris in tears. She was alone, and said that Crowley had made his escape by going out the front door.

The bartender was taken into custody and was yesterday arraigned before Justice Duffy, in the Essex Market Police Court. The girl told her story to the magistrate, and Blint, the prisoner, was held for examination without bail. Miss Joyce was a witness. She corroborated the story told by the complainant, and further stated that Crowley attempted to treat her in the same manner about six months ago.

"Are you sure it was Sergt. Crowley who took this girl to the bar room?" asked the Justice of another witness.

"Yes, your Honor," he replied; "I know him too well to be mistaken."

The Justice satisfied himself that Sergt. Crowley was the man he wanted and he immediately issued a warrant for his arrest. He gave it to Sergt. Cahill, of the Essex Market squad, to execute.

"I want you to find this man," said the magistrate, "and place him under arrest as soon as you find him."

Sergt. Cahill went to No. 293 Madison-street, where Crowley resides with his wife and three children. There he learned that the object of his search was on duty in the Thirty-fifth Precinct. Superintendent Walling was notified and he telegraphed to Crowley, asking him to appear at once at Police Headquarters. The request was complied with, and when Crowley arrived at the Central Office Sergt. Cahill was there and at once took him into custody. He appeared to be surprised, and said that was the first he knew of any such charge being made against him.

"This is the work of Hodden and Leary," he said, meaning Capt. Hedden and Detective Leary, of the Seventh Precinct. "I'll get square with them."

Crowley sent to George Rückert, the proprietor of the Summit Hotel, at the Bowery and Canal-street, and asked him to go bail. Rückert, however, failed to comply with the request, and the prisoner spent last night in Police Headquarters.

"The charge against me," he said, "is not true. I was at Standard Hall, however, in East Broadway, last night. I stopped there on my way home. I was introduced to a girl I don't know, as I never saw her before or since. I didn't ask her to drink or dance, as I am not a dancing man. I have no knowledge of the complaint preferred against me, and I first learned of it when the 'Super' (referring to Superintendent Walling) told me of it, after being sent for. You may depend on it I will prove my innocence when the proper time comes."

Crowley was appointed on the force in 1876 by Commissioner Wheeler, and was assigned to special duty. Previous to this he was a Deputy United States Marshal under John I. Davenport. Through the influence of Joel B. Erhardt and Col. George Bliss he was afterward made Sergeant and transferred from the Central Office to the Seventeenth Precinct. He had never worn the uniform of a patrolman. After serving in the Seventeenth Precinct he made a request to be transferred to the Seventh, and it was granted. During his sojourn in the Seventh Precinct he made himself very unpopular with the men under him. For political reasons he worked in the interest of the notorious border gang. When one of these men would get into trouble his friends would immediately look for Crowley, and the Sergeants in the Seventh Precinct say they were continually annoyed by the visits of these objectionable characters.

While under the influence of liquor Crowley once discharged his revolver at a patrolman, and the ball is still lodged in the frame of the door of the sitting room of the Madison-street station. In the early part of last March Officer Michael Rohan went behind the desk while Crowley was on duty. This displeased the Sergeant, and he showed evidence of his displeasure by kicking, punching, and finally attempting to shoot the patrolman. For this he was tried by the Commissioners. He was fined 10 days' pay and transferred to the Thirty-fifth Precinct. Crowley has several times escaped fines and perhaps dismissal on account of his powerful political friends. One of Crowley's children is named after Col. George Bliss, and only a short time ago the latter sent the child a handsome birthday present in the shape of a massive silver goblet. Crowley will be arraigned in the Essex Market Police Court to-day.

The Arraignment

Bliss arrived bruised and limping, his coat torn, one eye nearly closed.

"Don't say a word, Dave," he whispered. "They've already written the ending."

Mary sent a lawyer. His daughter brought a sandwich wrapped in wax paper that he couldn't stomach. A few allies promised support.

Then vanished.

"Everyone who touches you burns," Bliss said, voice like gravel.

Rickert, the banker who'd once hosted reformer fundraisers, promised bail.

Never showed.

Crowley spent that night beneath Mulberry Street in a holding cell with a dead bulb and the stink of rat piss and rusted iron.

He didn't sleep.

He didn't speak.

He just calculated.

They hadn't come to ruin his name.

They'd come to erase the man who still remembered the real ledger.

Three Weeks Later

The Trial Begins.

Chapter 36
The Trial

April – May 1885 | Manhattan Criminal Court

The courtroom was a coffin made of marble.

High ceilings. Oak benches. A crucifix above the judge's bench that no one dared look at too long.

By the time the trial began, Crowley was no longer a man.

He was a story, already written, already told.

The Herald called it "the case of the decade."

The Tribune ran Maggie's name beside headlines usually reserved for archbishops and murderers.

The World called it "justice long denied."

The prosecution walked in with clean coats and clean consciences.

The defense? Hired by Mary. Paid with borrowed funds. Half a step behind from the first gavel strike.

Day One , Selection

The jury was built for burning.

A glove-maker from Hester Street who nodded every time Maggie's name was mentioned.

A baker who once ran for alderman on a Tammany ticket.

Two men who worked city contracts Crowley had audited in 1881.

The defense protested.

The judge, a man whose election had been bankrolled by Kelly's slate, smiled.

"Overruled," he said.

That word would become a chorus.

Day Two , Maggie

She entered the courtroom like a lamb.

Pale blue dress. Hair tied with a white ribbon. She hadn't cried yet. They saved that for the stand.

When she swore her oath, the room stilled.

She told the story just as she'd been taught: the glove, the smile, the kind words, the request to walk downstairs. Then the darkness. The locked door. His breath on her neck. The sobs.

She didn't have to prove it.

She just had to paint it.

Her tears came exactly three minutes in. She clutched the Bible like a lifeline and stared at the jury with those trembling eyes.

Crowley watched from behind his own eyes, still and silent.

His attorney objected, asked why there was no sign of struggle, why the door had no lock, why no one heard a thing.

"Objection sustained," the judge said, but glared at the defense.

The damage had already been done.

Day Four , Disintegration

Witnesses who had vouched for Crowley during the Standard Hall investigation couldn't recall key details.

One claimed to have seen Crowley "tipsy."

Another said he'd *"lingered too long"* near the staircase.

The bartender? Gone.

The doorman? Dead two weeks before the trial.

The matron? Reassigned, unavailable.

One witness claimed Crowley left with Maggie.

Under oath, she faltered, but the jury didn't seem to notice.

Day Six , Crowley Testifies

It was a risk.

Bliss told him not to.

"They'll twist your words."

But Crowley had to look those twelve strangers in the eyes.

"I didn't touch that girl. I didn't enter that room. I came to that dance on a lead. The man I sought wasn't there. I left. That's the truth."

He said it simply.

No drama. No rage.

He just told the truth like it was a ledger only he could read.

The prosecutor smiled. Then asked about 1878. About the revolver incident. The time he pushed a superior officer. The time he was suspended.

They dragged up thirty years of service and painted them like sins.

The jury didn't flinch.

Final Day , Verdict

The deliberation lasted ninety-four minutes.

Crowley sat in his seat, motionless, staring through the floor like he could see the buried bones beneath the courthouse.

They returned with a single word:

Guilty.

Seventeen and a half years.

No parole recommendation.

Immediate transfer to Sing Sing.

The Aftermath

Mary wept quietly.

His daughter didn't make eye contact.

Bliss punched a wall in the corridor, fracturing two knuckles.

As they shackled Crowley and led him away, the bailiff whispered:

"Keep your head down in Ossining, Crowley. They eat cops alive."

Crowley didn't respond.

But as he passed through the rear hallway, past a forgotten janitor's closet, he slid a folded paper from his sleeve and dropped it behind a radiator.

A map.

A name.

A start.

Because this wasn't the end.

It was just the first blow in his war underground.

Chapter 37
Ashes to Ashes

April 1885 | Grand Central Station → Sing Sing Prison

The morning air at Grand Central was thick with coal smoke and judgment.

It was precisely 9:15 a.m. when David Crowley stepped onto the platform, flanked by marshals, wrists cuffed in front of him. The polished boots of the station guards rang against marble tile like funeral bells. A modest crowd had gathered, not to protest, not to gawk, but to witness.

To make sure he was really gone.

George Bliss was there.

Of course he was.

His suit was wrinkled. His collar torn. His face still bore the remnants of the alley fight he'd lost trying to hold the system together. He didn't offer pity. Just a cigar.

Crowley took it with his manacled hands. Bliss held out a match. No words. Just fire.

A small, shared defiance. A last indulgence.

Crowley drew once, twice, the smoke curling from his lips like a ghost of who he used to be. His eyes flicked toward the edge of the crowd: his sister, red-eyed and shaking. His brother, pale. His father, stoic, immovable, nodded once. But that single nod cracked something in Crowley's chest.

The train hissed into the station.

The guards moved.

The crowd parted.

Crowley stepped forward, flicked the cigar into the tracks.

Ashes to ashes.

The Ride North

No one spoke.

The train carved its way up the Hudson like a blade through black silk. The river gleamed in the morning sun, indifferent. The guards didn't glance at him. Crowley stared out the window at trees just beginning to bud for spring.

He should've felt ruined.

Instead, he felt waiting.

He wasn't going to Sing Sing to die.

He was going to sharpen.

Arrival at Sing Sing

The prison rose like a stone mouth.

Thick-walled. Windowless. Built from its own rock. Even the air seemed to die at the gates.

The main yard was silent. Inmates in gray filed like ghosts across gravel paths. The guards wore blank expressions and belts heavy with keys. Nobody greeted him.

Convicts weren't welcomed.

They were catalogued.

Crowley was processed like a defective tool, stripped of his identity, his belongings, his name. He stood bare under the harsh glare of an oil lamp while a clerk scratched his height, weight, and "disposition" into a leather-bound registry.

He was issued a number, a uniform, and a cot in Block D, where they put former cops, snitches, and the politically radioactive.

Routine

The bell rang at 5:00 a.m. sharp.

Every day.

No exceptions.

Crowley was assigned to the quarry crew, the prison's hardest labor. Out past the yard, beyond the orchard of gallows rumors, he smashed stone for ten hours a day.

Winter wind peeled skin from the bone.

Summer sun cooked the marrow.

Men collapsed weekly. Some didn't rise.

But Crowley never wavered.

He worked in silence, every hammer swing a metronome. Every day measured by calluses and cracks in the quarry wall.

Meals were worse than war rations: black bread, sour broth, and meat that seemed carved from old boots. Water was rationed. Talking was forbidden.

Sunday brought chapel, a priest with trembling hands and a voice like sandpaper. Redemption was offered on script. Crowley knew the game. He'd played it from the other side.

He didn't ask for forgiveness.

He asked for focus.

Adaptation

Within weeks, he had a rhythm.

Within months, a system.

He learned who ran what: who controlled favors, who smuggled paper, who held grudges worth trading. He memorized guard schedules, studied inmate patterns, and mapped weaknesses in the walls, not to escape, but to survive.

And always, always, he wrote.

Not on paper.

In his head.

Every name. Every movement. Every pattern of corruption he'd uncovered in New York.

It was all still alive, inside him.

They'd buried the man.

But not the mission.

Not the memory.

And one day, when the gates opened,

He wouldn't just walk out.

He'd return like a storm.

And the city that forgot him would learn what it meant to erase the wrong man.

Chapter 38
The Spark Outside

1886–1887 | New York City, Albany, and Washington

Freedom wasn't found in courtrooms anymore.

Not for a man like David Crowley.

Not after Tammany had poisoned the well so thoroughly that even clean hands came up black.

Mary knew this.

So did George Bliss.

That's why they stopped trying to reopen the case.

Instead, they started working on something harder: a pardon.

Because exoneration required a miracle.

But mercy, mercy could be negotiated.

Mary Crowley hadn't visited Sing Sing in months.

Not because she'd given up, but because it wasn't safe.

Eyes followed her now.

Notes arrived with no signatures.

Once, she found her laundry cut into strips on the line.

She'd stopped attending church.

Stopped speaking to neighbors.

She walked with her head down and her back straight, carrying letters in her boot and names in her memory.

She worked behind the scenes, gathering affidavits, lining up testimony.

Women Crowley had protected. Families he'd helped. Civil clerks, laborers, and one drunken constable who finally confessed:

"They told me to say he left with the girl. I never saw it. I just… wanted to keep my pension."

That statement would disappear the next day.

But Mary had already copied it in her own hand.

She filed nothing. Trusted no one.

She carried the truth on onion-skin paper pressed into a false seam in her corset.

Bliss worked the other end of the line.

He still had his post, barely. Every week was a new balancing act: pretending loyalty to the machine while planting doubt in the right rooms.

He met men on park benches. Slid packets under ledgers. Whispered in cloakrooms and across billiard tables.

The names he gathered were cautious but growing:

- **Elihu Root**, razor-sharp and already sniffing out corruption in federal contracts.
- **Joel Erhardt**, rising through the customs house, a clean man in a dirty system.
- **Daniel Sickles**, the one-legged general who had killed a man in Lafayette Park and walked away a hero. Sickles had always liked Crowley, once calling him "a gentleman with steel under his skin."

"These things take time," Bliss told Mary during one of their rare meetings, this one in a butcher's stall on Delancey.

"But there are cracks forming. Men with pull are starting to whisper."

Mary didn't smile. She just nodded.

Inside the Walls

Inside Sing Sing, Crowley felt the shift.

Not outwardly, the guards were no kinder, the food no better, the days no shorter.

But whispers reached him.

A warden's clerk left a law book in his cell, accidentally, he said.

Inside it: a dog-eared page on wrongful convictions and the procedural weight of governor's pardons.

Crowley studied it like a map.

He consumed legal texts, memorized criminal codes, learned the machinery that had chewed him up.

He mapped every moving part of the system that had buried him, and learned how each gear could be reversed.

Not that it made the time easier.

Men around him broke.

Some from the quarry. Some from the cellar beatings. Some from the silence.

But Crowley kept his footing.

Not because he was stronger.

Because he was sharpening.

A man like Crowley, educated, military-trained, law enforcement pedigree, should have cracked under the weight of injustice.

But he didn't.

He fought only when cornered.

Worked the jobs. Kept his eyes cold.

And over time, even the killers learned:

Crowley wasn't prey.

He was something else.

Something the prison couldn't quite reach.

The Spark

Years bled. Then years bled again.

The number of men who believed in him could be counted on one hand.

But they were the right men.

And outside the walls, the first cracks were forming.

Crowley didn't pray anymore.

Not to gods.

Not to presidents.

Not even to fate.

But every night before he closed his eyes, with the stench of rust and blood thick in the air, he whispered the same words like armor:

Not finished. Not yet.

Chapter 39
The Governor's Dilemma

November 1889 | Albany, New York & Sing Sing Prison

Governor Roswell P. Flower sat at his desk, a glass of untouched scotch sweating beside his elbow, and a letter trembling ever so slightly in his hand.

Outside the windows, Albany wore its November coat, slate sky, early frost. Inside, a roaring fire did nothing to shake the chill pressing down on him.

The letter before him had no seal of office. No formal complaint.

But it had teeth.

"Sergeant David Crowley's conviction is a miscarriage of justice."

"Evidence was falsified."

"Tammany Hall's fingerprints are all over this."

He had read it three times already, and each time the words burned deeper.

Flower wasn't naïve. He knew the courts were only as clean as the hands that counted votes. And Tammany's hands were everywhere.

But this wasn't just another plea from a prisoner crying innocence. This letter carried an implication too sharp to ignore:

The law had been twisted. Deliberately.

And it had happened under his watch.

An hour later, three men entered his private chamber.

No press. No staff. Just Elihu Root, Joel Erhardt, and George Bliss, whose jaw still carried the scar from Cherry Street, where Tammany's warning had found him.

Root didn't waste time.

He laid out the case like a surgeon preparing to cut:

1. A sworn affidavit from a former Tammany precinct captain naming Leary, Hedden, and Flynn in a premeditated setup.

2. A fragment of a ledger matching Crowley's original notes, cataloging construction fraud tied to city contracts.

3. A handwritten retraction from Maggie Morris, now living in Trenton under another name, admitting she had lied under pressure and been paid for her perjury.

"They rehearsed it. Said he'd ruined everything. That if I helped, I'd save my family. I didn't know what I was doing until it was too late."

The signature was shaky. The notary authentic.

Flower rubbed his eyes. "Jesus," he muttered. "You're telling me we convicted a man on the word of a coached girl, and burned the evidence."

Root's reply was sharp enough to draw blood.

"No, Governor. You let Tammany do it for you."

The silence that followed wasn't peaceful.

It was political.

Flower looked toward the fire, its light flickering over the piles of unsigned decrees and correspondence. He saw the headlines before they were written. He saw the blowback, the donors lost, the senators circling.

And he saw something else.

He saw a man in gray, pacing a cell upstate.

A man the system had tried to erase.

A man who had kept his mouth shut even after the cell door slammed.

Bliss broke the silence. His voice was quieter than the fire's crackle.

"Tammany will crucify you, Governor."

Flower didn't answer right away.

Then Bliss leaned closer, his scar catching the light.

"They already crucified Crowley."

The Decision

Hours after they left, Flower remained alone with the papers. The scotch had gone warm, untouched. The fire guttered low.

Duty warred with survival across his face.

He knew what signing the document would cost him. The machine would turn on him, slowly at first, then all at once. Patronage, appointments, campaign money, the quiet favors that made the Capitol run, they would vanish overnight.

But so would his reflection if he didn't.

Finally, he reached for the pen.

The nib trembled once, then steadied.

And with three strokes, Roswell P. Flower placed his name beneath the words:

"Executive Order of Clemency."

Sing Sing Prison , The Petition

Inside Sing Sing, David Crowley knew none of this.

The quarry still waited.

The food still bled the taste of rust and resignation.

But one morning, a guard approached with a folded letter, official, crested.

Crowley hesitated before taking it.

Inside: a petition. Signed by Bliss, Erhardt, Sickles, Root, and at the very bottom:

Governor Roswell P. Flower.

His hands trembled.

Not from cold, but from something far rarer in that place.

A flicker.

A flare.

Hope.

He didn't cry.

He didn't smile.

He just read the Governor's name again.

And then he whispered to himself, over and over, the words that had carried him through the quarry and the silence:

"Not finished. Not yet."

Chapter 40
The Final Push

July 1889, Albany and New York City

The days that followed Governor Flower's decision were thick with tension, political maneuvering, and whispers traded in backrooms like contraband.

The commission had been formed, the first real, tangible sign that David Crowley's long march toward justice might reach its end.

But the warning signs were already flashing: Tammany Hall would not surrender its grip easily.

The commission was lean by design, five men, all allegedly immune to politics.

But in a city like New York, where power fed on secrecy, no man was truly beyond reach.

Judge Charles H. Smith, a man with a reputation for incorruptibility, chaired the panel. Yet even he knew the dangers.

Tammany's reach was like smoke, it found cracks in every room, it curled around every word.

At Sing Sing, Crowley knew little of what was moving beyond the gates, but he felt the air change.

The guards grew quieter around him.

The warden didn't meet his eye.

When the morning roll call came, his name was spoken a little softer.

He didn't trust it. Not yet.

Then one afternoon, a familiar silhouette appeared in the visiting chamber. George Bliss, grayer, thinner, but with the same fire behind his eyes.

He placed a single document between them.

"The commission's begun," Bliss said. "But David... this will not be fast, and it will not be clean. Croker is already working every judge, every clerk. He's got half the city's printers on retainer."

Crowley scanned the page: official commission seal, language dressed in legal caution, intent buried in bureaucracy.

"You're saying they're stalling."

"They're suffocating it. One delay at a time."

Bliss leaned closer.

"But we've got cracks forming. There's an anonymous statement, alleges perjury by the O girl."

Crowley didn't blink.

"Maggie."

"A former housemaid says she was paid to lie about seeing you enter the room. O was coached. The timelines don't match. The building layout changed just before the incident, they claimed you locked a door that no longer existed."

Crowley's hands curled into fists.

"It was all theater. A damn play."

"Yes. And it's unraveling. We just need time."

Before leaving, Bliss offered one final warning.

"They're trying to shake Root. Pressure on Flower is brutal. Threats. Promises. Even bribes. But Root won't budge. And

Sickles is speaking to the press, calling your case the moral albatross of New York."

Crowley said nothing, but something in his chest shifted, like a lock beginning to turn.

Across the city, Tammany Hall burned with fury.

Richard Croker was livid.

The headlines were tightening.

The commission had subpoenaed payrolls, plumbing contracts, and voter registration logs. They were triangulating patterns of fraud, and Crowley's name was the thread.

"If Crowley walks," Croker snarled to Big Jim Carney, "it's not just him. It's us. Our people. Our system. He becomes a martyr, and we become parasites."

Croker's retaliation came fast.

Men who had once testified against Crowley were "visited."

A journalist investigating the sewer contracts vanished for three days, returning with bruises and no memory.

Still, the commission pushed forward.

They interviewed the former prison chaplain.

They unearthed a ledger once thought lost, Delaney's book, the one Crowley had sworn existed.

A single surviving page matched his handwriting.

Governor Flower received nightly reports.

Each more damning than the last.

And then came the final blow:

A signed affidavit from Maggie Morris, now twenty-three, living quietly in Connecticut.

"I was coerced," it read. "I was threatened. The story I gave was not my own."

That was it.

Flower read it alone, at midnight, under lamplight.

The political fallout would be enormous.

But there was no longer any question.

Crowley had been buried alive by a system that mistook silence for guilt.

And now,

the machine would face its reckoning.

Chapter 41
The Last Gambit

Wednesday November 22 1893, Albany and New York City

The storm was coming. David Crowley felt it in the marrow of his bones. The days inside Sing Sing had grown restless. Guards spoke in clipped whispers, and even the prisoners sensed the shift. The air held weight, like the world was about to tip.

Weeks had passed since the commission had begun peeling back the lies. Now the whispers came faster, more urgent. Something was about to break.

But Crowley wasn't naïve. He knew the nature of the beast. Tammany Hall didn't lose. It devoured, adapted, and struck from the shadows.

In the heart of Manhattan, Richard Croker stood at the helm of the beast: its new boss, its cleaner, its knife. Croker had tried political charm, legal bribes, and judicial favors. But now, with the commission closing in and the Governor wavering toward pardon, Croker reached into his darkest drawer.

He summoned Marcus "Mad Dog" O'Neill.

O'Neill had no office, no official title. He was Croker's butcher, broad-shouldered, balding, always chewing the stub of a cigar. A man who solved problems by making them disappear.

"Stop the commission," Croker growled, his voice tight with fury. "If they free Crowley, the papers will crucify us. Burn it down if you have to."

Mad Dog smiled with his teeth.

Meanwhile, in Albany, Governor Roswell P. Flower sat in his chambers, staring at the affidavit from Maggie Morris. Her confession had shifted everything. The commission had done its job. But the pressure was unbearable.

Tammany's reach curled around his office like smoke under a door. Political allies warned him: back off or be buried.

He didn't listen.

But Flower knew what was coming. The threats. The deals. The violence.

He called in security. Then he called George Bliss.

By that evening, a carriage was on its way to Sing Sing.

Crowley didn't ask questions when they pulled him from his cell. He saw the closed carriage waiting beyond the gate and knew something had changed.

"Get in," Bliss said. His face was pale, his eyes bloodshot.

"What's going on?"

"O'Neill. Croker sent him. They're moving now. If we don't get to Flower tonight, it might be too late."

As the carriage sped north, Bliss briefed him.

Tammany had bribed three of the five commissioners. One had disappeared. The Governor's aides had been bought or threatened. Even Elihu Root had received a bullet casing in the mail.

In the dark alleys of the city, O'Neill's men were making their final push. Witnesses were intimidated. One clerk was found floating in the Hudson. Another, the stenographer who took Maggie Morris's first statement, had vanished.

Bliss handed Crowley a sealed letter. "It's a declaration. Signed by Root, Sickles, and Erhardt. If Flower delays, we release it to every paper from here to Washington. The whole machine burns."

By midnight, they arrived at the Governor's mansion.

The mansion was under guard. Inside, Flower looked ten years older. His hand trembled as he held the affidavit, the evidence from the commission, and the letter Bliss had just delivered.

"They said they'd ruin me," Flower whispered.

"They already have," Crowley said. "You just don't know it yet. But if you sign that pardon, Governor, if you do the right thing, you won't be remembered for the dirt they dragged you through. You'll be remembered for pulling New York out of its filth."

There was silence.

Then Flower picked up the pen.

He signed.

That night, as Crowley stepped into the cold air, free for the first time in nearly a decade, he didn't smile.

He lit a match. Watched it burn.

The war wasn't over.

But the reckoning had begun.

Chapter 42
The Cost of Freedom

Thursday November 23 1893 , New York City

The train hissed into Grand Central at precisely 10:30 a.m., dragging its breath of steam and coal grime from the Hudson Valley. The platform bustled with holiday travelers, but for one man, the moment was heavier than any homecoming parade.

David Crowley stepped down like a ghost reentering the world, accompanied by Geroge Bliss. Eight years behind stone walls had not broken him, though they had left their mark. His borrowed coat sagged on his shoulders, his shoes were scuffed, but his eyes, gray, sharp, unwavering, burned with the fire of a man who had survived both iron bars and betrayal.

Waiting for them was Sergeant George Little, long retired but still ramrod straight, his fists clenched against the chill. Crowley's first mentor, the man who had once taught him how to settle disputes with fists before paperwork, stood at the foot of the platform. Their handshake was wordless and crushing, the kind of silent recognition shared only by men who had survived different kinds of war.

They walked together to the stationhouse in the same building, no escort, no speeches, no bands, just a quiet return to a city that had moved on without him. Some of the officers on duty stiffened when he entered. A few offered nods, others cautious handshakes, most simply stared at the man who had gone down so hard and come back scarred, but not erased.

By noon, Crowley had slipped into the bloodstream of the city, vanishing into the screech and jostle of the Third Avenue Elevated. The train rattled north through smoke and soot, past tenement roofs and church spires, carrying him toward the

Bronx. His stop was 231 Willis Avenue, a second-floor walk-up that was now home.

When the door swung open, the smell of stove coal and fresh bread struck him like a wave of memory. Mary Agnes Crowley stood framed in the doorway, the woman who had never flinched, never petitioned for annulment, never once signed her name without his. She wrapped her arms around him before he could speak. Her tears came first, his followed, and then their children, hesitant at first, grown older than when he had left, joined in the embrace.

In that small kitchen, the war receded for one blessed hour. The turkey was dry, the gravy too thick, but it was Thanksgiving, and Crowley ate not from a prison tin but at his family's table. Later, on the stoop with Mary, he sipped black coffee and watched the leaves spiral from the trees. For the first time in nearly a decade, the future seemed possible again.

Friends gathered in the parlor, a few loyal souls who had never believed the headlines. They pressed a cigar into his hand. He lit it slowly, exhaling as if daring the world to interrupt his first real breath of freedom.

Outside, reporters had already begun to circle. When they caught him later that afternoon, he stood steady, his cigar still glowing.

"I have nothing to say just at present," he told them. "But it won't be long before I do. And something that may make a little stir."

Then he turned, nodding to Mary. "That woman never doubted me. Not once in eight years. And for those who spread rumors about divorce, she stayed. When the world turned its back, she didn't."

He had no job, no uniform, no clear plan. But Crowley wasn't idle. Prison had taught him patience, and now he would wield it like a weapon.

The crime that had stolen eight years of his life, the alleged assault of Maggie Morris, a sixteen-year-old shopgirl, during a ball on East Broadway, still clung to him like a shadow. The newspapers had devoured it, The World above all, peddling every lurid detail. Within three weeks he had been arrested, tried in General Sessions, and sentenced to seventeen years.

The presiding judge had been Recorder Smyth. The prosecutor: De Lancey Nicoll. Both men ambitious. Both tied to Tammany Hall.

Crowley had maintained his innocence from the start. Maggie Morris had lied, he said, or worse, she had been used, a pawn in a machine that wanted him silenced.

And yet, it was not lawyers who freed him. It was a name. General Daniel Sickles.

Decades earlier, Crowley had served Sickles when he was still just a wiry courthouse runner. Sickles had needed a boy reckless enough to climb an iron pipe and slip a writ through Jay Gould's barricaded doors. Crowley had done it without blinking. Sickles had laughed and told him: "You ever need a favor, you come to me."

He hadn't forgotten.

When the pardon petition landed on Governor Roswell P. Flower's desk in late 1892, it carried not only Sickles's signature, but also those of Nicoll, the very prosecutor who had convicted him, and Smyth, the judge who had sentenced him. Together, they cracked the door open. Governor Flower signed the pardon.

On December 1, 1893, the New York Times headline blazed:

DAVID H. CROWLEY AGAIN FREE. THE EX-SERGEANT OF POLICE WILL SOON SEEK TO PROVE HIS INNOCENCE.

That night, whiskey in hand, George Little sat across from him at the kitchen table. The two men spoke little, as was their way. When the silence grew long, Crowley leaned forward, his voice low and steady.

"There's a reckoning coming."

Little nodded, eyes narrowing. "Then we'd best be ready."

Tammany was not gone. Richard Croker still pulled the strings from his oak-paneled rooms. Maggie Morris had vanished. Files had been buried. Evidence suppressed. But David Crowley was no longer inmate #3467. He was free. And he had eight years of patience, sharpened like a blade, waiting for the first strike.

Chapter 43
The Hearth

December 1893, Willis Avenue, The Bronx

The house on Willis Avenue was not much to look at, two floors of weathered brick above a bakery, the windows rattling in the winter wind, but to David Crowley, it was a palace. Every creak in the floorboards, every hiss of the coal stove, every scuff of the children's boots across the hall was a symphony compared to the silence of Sing Sing.

He rose early, long before the others stirred, and stood at the window with a cup of coffee Mary had pressed into his hands. The city outside was a restless beast, but here, in the second-floor flat, he felt something close to peace. Mary came behind him and wrapped her arms around his waist. He held her hands against his chest, as if by clutching them he could keep the years from slipping away again.

"You never changed," he whispered.

She laughed softly. "I did. But you... you stayed with me."

At breakfast, the children stole glances at him, as though testing whether he was real. George Bliss, no longer the boy he remembered but a young man with his father's jaw, asked careful questions about prison life, then quickly changed the subject when he saw the shadows in his father's eyes. The youngest, a daughter who had been too small to remember him, reached across the table and simply placed her hand in his. Crowley swallowed hard and kissed her knuckles.

Meals became a ritual. No wardens barking orders, no tin trays, no watery soup ladled from iron pots. Instead, there was the smell of bread baking in the oven, the scrape of chairs on wood, the arguments over who would fetch the butter. Every bite reminded him of what he had lost, and every smile reminded him that not everything had been taken.

On Sunday, Mary insisted they walk to Mass together. Arm in arm, they moved down Willis Avenue, neighbors stepping aside, whispering. Some nodded politely, others crossed the street. Crowley felt their stares but kept his gaze ahead. The children walked close, protective in their own way. Inside the church, when the congregation rose to sing, Crowley's voice broke on the first verse. Mary's hand tightened on his.

At night, after the children slept, the house grew quiet save for the ticking of the mantel clock. Crowley would sit with Mary by the stove, a shawl across her shoulders, his cigar glowing faintly in the dark. They talked in fragments, about rent, about school, about whether the boy might join the police someday. But always, the talk circled back to them.

"I thought of you every night," he told her once. "Every single night. It was the only way to stay alive."

Mary brushed the gray from his temple and kissed him like she had on their wedding day, as if time itself had bent and given them a second chance.

For a few weeks, life was almost ordinary. Crowley walked the children to school, carried coal up the narrow stairs, even fixed the squeaky hinge on the kitchen door. He laughed louder than he had in years. Mary said he looked younger each day, as though the prison years were retreating from his face.

But when the house grew still and the city's hum pressed through the window, the old fire returned to his eyes. He would sit in the dark, staring at nothing, remembering names, remembering voices in the courtroom, remembering Maggie Morris.

Mary knew not to disturb him when the silence came. She would set her hand lightly on his shoulder, and he would return to her, always.

For now, there was peace. For now, there was family.

And though the reckoning waited, David Crowley let himself believe, if only in stolen moments, that home was enough.

Chapter 44
Smoke and Sparks

December 1893, New York City

Freedom was a dangerous gift. David Crowley knew that now.

It had only been three weeks since his release, and already the city had begun to whisper again. Some called him a symbol. Others, a threat. Most weren't sure which. But Crowley didn't care what they called him. He hadn't endured eight years of stone and silence just to fade back into anonymity. He had work to do. War to finish.

The political fallout from his exoneration had detonated across New York like a barrel of dry powder. Newspapers that once buried him now trumpeted his release with suspicious enthusiasm. The Herald ran a three-column feature titled: "Crowley Rises: A Machine's Mistake?" while The World, not to be outdone, floated rumors of a civil suit against the city for wrongful imprisonment. Even The Times, usually immune to spectacle, published an editorial questioning the integrity of Recorder Smyth and De Lancey Nicoll, both of whom had recanted their earlier certainty in private letters.

But it wasn't the press that worried Tammany.

It was the people.

Irish dockworkers raised their pints in his honor. Former cops shook his hand on street corners. And in the neighborhoods where the political machine had long bought silence with soup kitchens and Christmas turkeys, Crowley's name was now spoken with something that sounded dangerously like hope.

Richard Croker watched it all unfold from his Fifth Avenue parlor, the velvet curtains drawn tight. He held a tumbler of scotch in one hand and a list in the other, Crowley sightings, meetings, conversations.

"He's building something," Croker muttered to Big Jim Carney, his ever-present fixer.

"A story, maybe," Carney said. "But stories don't stick unless you write them in blood."

Croker smiled. "Then maybe it's time we sharpened our pens."

Meanwhile, Crowley was already in motion.

He met with Elihu Root in a small backroom office above a printing shop in the East Village. Root brought more than legal skill; he brought names.

"These men were at the center of it all," Root said, spreading a list across the table. "Judges. Clerks. Detectives who signed affidavits under oath. Contractors who helped launder campaign money."

Crowley didn't blink. "We publish it. All of it. Anonymous. Piece by piece. We turn the machine on itself."

"And what happens when they come for you again?" Root asked.

"Then we're doing it right."

He also reconnected with Joel Erhardt, who had quietly risen to influence in municipal reform circles. Through him, Crowley gained access to donors, organizers, and newspapers sympathetic to the anti-Tammany cause. Sickles had already begun whispering in Washington. Crowley's name was being mentioned not just as a victim, but as a possible candidate.

Not yet, he thought. Not until the truth is laid bare.

His first official act wasn't a rally or a lawsuit. It was a funeral.

Patrick Delaney's grave had gone unmarked since his murder in 1884. Crowley paid out of pocket for a headstone.

The inscription read: "Friend. Ledger Keeper. Loyal to the End."

At the ceremony, George Bliss stood beside him. When it ended, Bliss turned to him and said, "You really plan to take them down, don't you?"

"Not just take them down," Crowley said. "Burn the roots."

Behind them, a small group of reporters lingered. One approached.

"Mr. Crowley, will you be running for office?"

Crowley smiled, thin and sharp. "Not yet. First, I have a city to clean."

The war had entered its next phase.

Not in the courts. Not in the streets

But in the shadows. Where power hid.

Where Crowley now hunted.

Chapter 45
The Judas File

January 1894, New York City

The Judas File wasn't just a list. It was a reckoning.

Crowley held the thick leather folio in his hands like a loaded weapon. Inside: names, signatures, memoranda. Testimonies buried. Evidence tampered with. A timeline of betrayal, sealed and stamped in the bureaucratic ink of Tammany Hall.

He didn't find it. It found him.

George Bliss delivered it in a brown paper envelope, eyes bloodshot, jaw clenched like he'd bitten down on something bitter and permanent.

"Where did it come from?" Crowley asked.

Bliss didn't blink. "Think of it as penance. From someone who knows they're running out of time."

The file had been stolen from the city comptroller's private safe. It traced payoffs from a network of city inspectors, legal clerks, and even parish priests back to a single ledger: the one Delaney died trying to protect.

Bliss watched as Crowley leafed through the pages. "You need to understand something. This doesn't just expose corruption, it implicates everyone. Judges. Cops. Priests. The girl."

"Maggie Morris?"

Bliss nodded. "There's a memo from a Tammany solicitor confirming a payment to her uncle days before the trial. A property deed transfer, upstate. It's buried in Section D."

Crowley's jaw tightened. His voice turned low, icy. "She was a child. A pawn they fed to the fire."

"She was used. We both were."

Crowley closed the folio and set it on the desk with reverence and fury. "No more hiding. No more caution. We open this vein and let the city bleed."

Meanwhile, Elihu Root had gone silent. Not out of fear, but calculation. He had seen the file and knew its gravity.

"If this leaks," Root said, arms crossed in his law office off Park Row, "it could decapitate the machine. But it could also trigger riots."

"Then we don't leak it," Crowley replied, voice edged like a blade. "We aim it. Like a rifle. Like a promise."

Root paused, then nodded. "Let me draft the first subpoenas. And David, keep a close eye on your allies. This kind of truth makes men disappear."

Across the city, Richard Croker stood in his study, the gaslight flickering over oak-paneled walls. He had just received word from his courier, the Judas File existed. Worse, it was no longer in city hands.

"Bliss," Croker growled. "That slippery bastard."

Big Jim Carney stood nearby, arms folded. "What do you want to do?"

"Silence them. Legally, if we can. Otherwise... otherwise."

But Croker had another problem. Daniel Sickles. The old general had begun to speak publicly, editorials, telegrams to Washington, whispers in the War Department. He'd called Crowley's conviction "the gravest domestic betrayal since Booth." Sickles had nothing to lose. A war hero, a scandal survivor, and a man with a long memory.

"You remember when that boy crawled up a pipe to serve Jay Gould?" Sickles said in one letter to The Herald. "That was Crowley. And now he's climbing again, this time to pull the leeches off the city's throat."

And Maggie Morris? She was still missing. Or hiding. One letter had surfaced in Connecticut, unsigned, but heartbreakingly candid.

"They made me lie. I was only sixteen. They told me he'd hurt others if I didn't. That I'd go to jail. I'm sorry."

It was enough. More than enough.

By the month's end, Crowley had assembled a private task force, volunteer lawyers, investigators, even a few repentant city clerks. They worked from a tenement loft on 14th Street, its door unmarked, its windows always shuttered.

Their mission? Dissect the Judas File. Expose Tammany. Make the first arrests.

Crowley stood before them, backlit by the cold winter sun slicing through the blinds. His words came slow and deliberate.

"This isn't about vengeance anymore," he said. "It's about restoration. We don't just want their heads, we want their system dismantled. We don't want justice in a courtroom. We want justice in the history books. This is our city, and it's time we took it back."

He paused, looked each of them in the eye. "They'll come after us. They'll call us traitors, criminals, anarchists. Let them."

He rested his hand on the folio. "This... this is our sword. And we use it. Not to threaten. Not to scare. To cut."

In that room, they drew up a name.

The first to fall.

And the fuse was lit.

Chapter 46
The Fallout

February 1894, New York City

The city was waking to a different kind of winter.

Snow fell over Manhattan like a shroud, softening the hard edges of rooftops and lamplight. But beneath the hush, something seethed. Tammany Hall had felt the tremor from the Judas File, and now the political ground was shifting. David Crowley had moved the first piece.

And now the machine moved to crush him.

Crowley knew it was coming. The day after his team selected the first name from the file, Alderman Henry Tilton, a Tammany bagman turned municipal contractor, a fire broke out in the records office of the Department of Streets and Sanitation. Three clerks were hospitalized. Two files were destroyed. One of them contained the original permits for Tilton's sewer bid.

"They're already erasing the trail," Crowley muttered, reading the headlines in The Herald. "They think fire can erase memory."

Bliss paced across the tenement floor like a wolf, his coat still dusted with snow. "Croker's rattled. He's tightening his grip, but he's bleeding allies. Root says Tilton's already fled to Boston."

Crowley looked to the corner, where the folio still sat on a locked desk. "Then he won't be the last."

But it wasn't just political files burning. Crowley's home on Willis Avenue was vandalized overnight. A brick through the window, wrapped in butcher paper: STAY DEAD. His son George found it before school. Mary didn't flinch.

"They're scared of what you know," she said, calmly sweeping glass into a dustpan. "Good."

At the Governor's Mansion in Albany, Roswell P. Flower was facing fire of a different sort. Tammany men were calling in debts, threatening legislative obstruction, and whispering of primary challengers. But the public was shifting. The editorials had changed tone. Sickles had seen to that.

The general now wrote under a pseudonym, "Horatius", penning op-eds that struck like bayonets. One appeared in the Tribune:

"The city burns not from chaos, but from cowardice. Crowley was not the exception. He was the beginning."

Croker convened his loyalists in a smoke-clogged clubroom on Lafayette Street. Big Jim Carney tossed a copy of the Tribune onto the table.

"They're turning him into a bloody folk hero."

Croker slammed a hand down. "Then we bury the legend."

He leaned in. "Find Maggie Morris."

Meanwhile, in the shuttered office on 14th Street, Crowley planned his next strike.

They had their opening. The Tilton evidence had been scrubbed from city records, yes, but Root had quietly obtained bank statements showing deposits that didn't match his salary. A subpoena was issued. The press would get the story within days.

And more were coming. Testimony from a court clerk confirming forged affidavits. A whistleblower from the Building Commission. A retired beat cop who'd seen payoffs change hands in Tammany saloons.

Crowley took them all in.

"This isn't a wave," he told Bliss that night. "It's a rising tide. And the machine doesn't know how to swim."

He paused at the window, watching the snow fall over the rooftops.

"They wanted me gone. Forgotten. Now they can't shut me up. And they sure as hell can't stop what's coming next."

He lit a cigar, the same way he had on the platform at Grand Central, weeks ago, and let the smoke curl toward the ceiling like a slow fuse.

Because war was coming.

Not with bullets.

With truth.

Chapter 47
The Hammer of Croker

May 1894, New York City

Richard Croker had built an empire with whispered favors and clenched fists. But now, as the Judas File spread like a toxin through the city's political bloodstream, Croker turned to the weapon he trusted most:

Fear.

It began quietly. A judge set to hear the Tilton subpoena case resigned without explanation. The replacement? A Tammany loyalist known more for horse racing debts than legal insight. A junior investigator on Crowley's task force slipped on ice outside his tenement door. A coincidence, the coroner said. But Bliss found bruises under the man's ribs.

By the second week of March, Croker stopped hiding. He moved operations to an apartment above a cigar parlor in Hell's Kitchen. No more backroom clubs or council halls. Here, men came in through the rear alley, past a drunk sleeping against the barrels. Inside, the wallpaper peeled and the smoke never cleared.

"Crowley thinks he can gut us like we're pigs," Croker said, stabbing a finger into the map of Manhattan. "But pigs don't run a city. We do."

Big Jim Carney leaned forward. "Then we hit back. Real hits."

Croker nodded once. "I want three things. First: find every man who signed that pardon petition. Ruin them. Publicly. Root's got a mistress in Brooklyn. Drag it into the papers. Sickles, drag up the old scandal, the murder, the affair. Anything."

"And the second?"

"Find O. If she's above ground, she talks. If she talks, he wins."

"And the third?"

Croker looked at a black ledger on the table. "Crowley's boy."

Carney blinked. "The kid?"

"No kid. A message. Crowley thinks he can protect his own? Let's see how long that lasts."

Meanwhile, Crowley moved his family under false names to a boarding house near Fordham. George was pulled from school. Mary wore a shawl in public. Every morning, Crowley walked them to the corner in silence, his eyes scanning for shadows.

At night, he returned to the war room.

The task force now had four new affidavits. A priest from St. Brigid's who admitted laundering funds for Alderman Tilton. A stenographer from General Sessions who saw the pages of Crowley's original testimony changed before filing. Even a retired Pinkerton who'd once been paid to "tail" Crowley and feed false reports to City Hall.

And still, it wasn't enough.

"We need O," Crowley told Bliss. "She's the hinge. If she speaks publicly, it's over for them."

"And if Croker finds her first?"

Crowley didn't answer. He didn't have to.

He stepped into the center of the room, rolled up his sleeves. His voice dropped low:

"We hit back. Not with threats. Not with knives. With truth so loud it deafens them."

He pulled a new document from his coat. A list of city properties flipped for profit by Tammany intermediaries. "This hits next week. The Times already has it. But that's not the real strike."

"What is?" Bliss asked.

Crowley smiled darkly.

"We make the people turn. We make the streets remember who owns them. And we make Richard Croker wish he'd left me in that cell."

In the shadows of City Hall, the whispers grew louder. The old alliances strained. District attorneys began refusing calls from Croker's men. A reporter from The Herald was found beaten under the Williamsburg Bridge. His notebook, gone.

Croker doubled his guards.

But it wasn't enough.

Because something worse than exposure had begun.

Momentum.

And it was on Crowley's side.

Chapter 48
The Rising Tide

January 1895, New York City

It began with a whisper.

Then a headline.

Then a march.

The Judas File was no longer just a dossier locked in Crowley's drawer. It was a reckoning. Every name that emerged dripped with scandal, graft, theft. Each release was surgical. A city contracts director tied to fraudulent fire escapes. A school board trustee skimming building funds. A judge who sold rulings for campaign donations.

By mid-April, the people were no longer watching passively. They were speaking. Demanding. Rising.

George Bliss stood at the front of a crowd outside City Hall, watching a wall of citizens clutching papers, placards, and outrage.

"Crowley lit the match," Bliss said, his voice barely audible over the chants. "We just threw it into the powder keg."

And above it all, Crowley watched from a rooftop across the street. His eyes scanned the square, jaw tight, coat whipping in the wind. Eight years in a cell had not prepared him for this: the thunder of the people on his side.

He turned to Root, who stood beside him, arms crossed.

"You still think justice comes in paper envelopes?" Crowley asked.

Root smirked. "Justice is a slow knife. But this, " he gestured toward the roar below ", this is a damn guillotine."

They had struck the city where it hurt: its shame.

But the cost was rising. Reporters covering the leaks were being followed. One was stabbed outside his boarding house. A friendly judge received a funeral wreath on his desk. Crowley's old precinct captain was found hanging in his barn, the note read like a warning, not a goodbye.

Even still, the tide rose.

Maggie Morris, the girl at the center of it all, had vanished. Rumors placed her in Ohio. Or Montreal. Or married under a false name in Boston. Crowley didn't know. And in quiet moments, he admitted to himself: he no longer needed her. Her silence had been Tammany's keystone. But now, the machine was crumbling under its own weight.

It was the people who were the lever now.

Crowley returned home that evening to laughter.

Mary was in the kitchen, sleeves rolled, face flushed with joy as George recited a passage from his school reader. He paused when he saw his father and ran to hug him, hard.

"They cheered for you today," George whispered. "At school. They said you're a hero."

Crowley crouched, pulled the boy close. "Heroes don't hide, son. But they do bleed. You remember that."

He rose, kissed Mary on the cheek. For one breathless moment, the world was right.

Then he looked at the window. Cracked. A pebble on the floor.

Another warning.

Bliss arrived minutes later, trench coat soaked. He pulled Crowley aside.

"Croker knows you're winning. He's panicking. I've got word he's preparing to flee to Europe. But before he does, he's going scorched earth."

Crowley didn't blink. "Let him burn the fields. I'm planting something else."

"What?"

Crowley opened his satchel. Inside: a fresh stack of papers. Next names. Next crimes. Next wave.

He handed Bliss the top page.

"Release it tomorrow. Let the city choke on its secrets."

That night, as Crowley walked home from a closed-door meeting with Root and Sickles, he noticed the streetlamps flickering dimly in the fog. He didn't see the men until it was too late.

Two shadows lunged from an alleyway. A blackjack cracked against his skull. Crowley staggered. The second blow drove him to his knees.

Boots. Fists. A knee to the ribs. He tasted blood.

"Message from Croker," one of them hissed. "Stay buried."

Then they vanished into the darkness, leaving Crowley bleeding on the cobblestones.

But he didn't stay down.

By dawn, his face was swollen, lip split, ribs aching, but his fire burned hotter. He stood before the press that afternoon, bandaged but unshaken.

"They tried to silence me," he said. "But the truth doesn't bruise. It doesn't bleed. And it doesn't back down."

He raised the next set of files. The Judas File wasn't finished.

Not even close.

In the alley below, two more watchers waited. But upstairs, a revolution was already roaring.

And it still had Crowley's name at the top.

Chapter 49
The Letters in Her Boot

April 1895 – Bronx, New York

The moment she heard the knock, Mary Crowley slid her hand beneath the floorboard.

Not for a weapon. For the envelope.

She knew that knock. Measured. Controlled. Three beats, then a pause. It wasn't the police, not yet, but it was someone close enough to smell the blood in the water. The Judas File had broken wide. Names were leaking. Ledgers missing. And every man who'd once whispered his loyalty to David was now stepping back into the fog.

Mary moved like she'd practiced. Because she had.

The kettle stayed on the stove. The newspaper folded just so. Her shawl draped across the rocker. The house had to look normal. Forgettable. A widow's home, nothing more. Not the last firewall between her husband's truth and Kelly's final lie.

She tucked the envelope into her left boot. Thin leather, worn at the heel, always too tight around the ankle. She'd sewn a slit behind the lining last spring, just wide enough for a folded document. Sometimes it was correspondence from Bliss. Sometimes a location. Sometimes it was just names. Tonight, it was everything.

She opened the door with a tired smile.

A man stood in the vestibule, hat low, collar up. He didn't offer a name.

"I believe you know my husband," she said softly.

"I know of him," the man replied. His hands were empty, but his eyes weren't. They scanned the room in quick sweeps, corners, mantels, shadows. "I'm just following up. Routine."

"Then we'll keep it routine."

She let him step inside, no more than three feet past the threshold. Her hands stayed at her sides, calm and plain. Just a woman holding a house together. That's what they saw, these men, when they even looked at all.

They never saw what she carried.

The visitor asked about David. His work. His health. His whereabouts.

Mary said he was traveling. Syracuse. A cousin's illness.

She lied cleanly.

She lied like someone who'd practiced in prayer.

And when he pressed, Has he been in contact? Are you in possession of any of his belongings?, she let her eyes widen just slightly. A widow's confusion.

"Sir... I wash laundry for neighbors to afford eggs. I don't keep ledgers."

He left after eight minutes.

She waited ten more before moving.

She didn't exhale until she was in the back pantry, alone, crouched beside the flour sacks. There, she removed her boot and pulled out the envelope. Still dry. Still sealed.

The Judas File wasn't just a name. It was a list. A slow bleed of false evidence planted to frame David's final downfall. Old colleagues were flipping. Bliss had gone silent. And one of the few copies of the real documents, the ones that proved the manipulation, was sitting in her boot, inside a pantry that smelled of yeast and damp stone.

She placed the envelope in the hollow behind the pantry wall. Replaced the board. Smoothed the flour sacks. Whispered a quiet Hail Mary.

And went to make tea.

Upstairs, George was reading by oil lamp. Lillian had moved out months ago, married now, with a baby on the way. The house felt too quiet. But Mary didn't let the silence win. She poured the tea, buttered bread, added sugar. Rituals mattered. Especially now.

Because if they came again, and they would, she'd need them to see nothing.

She was just a woman.

Just a mother.

Just a ghost of the story they thought they understood.

But in her boot, and in her bones, she carried what they could never burn.

Chapter 50
The Firewall

The Bronx – July 1895

There were days Mary couldn't recall the sound of her own voice.

Not the way it was now, thin, measured, soothing for others. But the voice she once used freely, sharp with wit, lit with conviction. She had once stood in a crowded church and recited vows with a heart that outran her breath. She had once stormed into precinct houses with a crying child on her hip, demanding her husband be released or at least allowed a fair hearing. She had once shouted into wind and street noise when the baby was late home from school.

But now, now she whispered.

To the children. To the walls. To the folded letters beneath the floorboards of the front parlor.

She was the firewall.

And she was holding.

The headlines were everywhere again.

CROWLEY JUDAS FILE WIDENS

RE-OPENED CHARGES MAY LEAD TO REVOCATION OF PARDON

WHISTLEBLOWER OR FRAUD?

David tried to shield the house from it, but papers made it in through the cracks. George found one folded into his lunch pail. Lillian overheard it at Mass. The whispers were too loud to silence.

David was unraveling. She could see it in his hands, fidgeting, always reaching for a ledger or a pen that wasn't there. He drank more coffee now, barely slept, paced at night with the steps of a man who used to march.

And yet, he would not stop.

So she would not either.

She retrieved the last batch of correspondence from the old shoemaker on O Avenue. Bliss had sent them under a false name, return address marked "Concordium Tailors", but she knew George's handwriting blindfolded. Inside were minutes from secret depositions, coded notes on shifting political alliances, and one name that made her blood run cold.

Malley.

She hadn't said the name in years. Not since the trial. Not since that day in Sing Sing when she saw him watching the train David had arrived on, smiling like a man who knew how stories ended.

The letter was brief. A single line:

"Malley is back in play. Possibly tied to the judiciary angle. Watch postmasters and clerks."

Mary folded the note once, twice, then tucked it in the worn lining of her boot beneath her long gray skirt. Her breath caught. Her legs didn't. She moved quickly.

She wasn't just hiding evidence. She was smuggling the defense.

That night, after the children were asleep, David sat hunched over the kitchen table, his back a coastline of years and weight. He didn't speak when she entered. Just passed her the latest affidavit from a former Tammany clerk who had suddenly gone mute again.

Fear, she thought. It moves faster than justice.

"I think I lost George Bliss," David said, voice low. "They're cutting lines. The ones we thought were safe."

Mary placed the kettle on the stove.

"You still have me," she said.

He nodded, but didn't meet her eyes.

After a moment, she reached beneath her apron and withdrew a folded sheet.

"What's this?" he asked, brow furrowed.

"Schedule of postal transfers from the Bronx to downtown," she said. "Your Judas file, one of them isn't routing through a court. It's going to a box owned by the State Political Committee. Malley's name was added as a 'reviewing officer' two weeks ago."

David looked up slowly.

"I tracked it through the baker's union manifest," she added. "Code's in the ledger. Back of the receipts. You've got six days."

He didn't speak.

So she leaned forward, placed her hand over his, and said it again, this time not as a wife, but as the only firewall left between her husband and history's erasure.

"You still have me."

Chapter 51
Judas in the Kitchen

August 1895 – The Bronx

The man was wearing her son's coat.

That was the first thing Mary noticed.

He stood at the kitchen table as if he belonged there, steam rising from the coffee cup in his hand. David's files lay open, open, before him: the red ledger, the affidavits, Bliss's most recent letter, still unfolded.

And he was wearing George's coat. Same patch on the elbow. Same missing button.

He looked up, startled, smiling too quickly.

"Aunt Mary," he said. "Didn't expect you back so soon."

Mary's heart clenched. Not Aunt. Not really. Not by blood.

But Joseph Joey Maloney had been around the family since his mother died, since David brought him in after the riot on Mott Street, since he started running errands for Bliss. David had trusted him.

So had she. Until now.

"What are you doing?" she asked quietly.

"David said I could warm up," he said, too casually. "I was just reviewing the files for him. Organizing."

"David is in Yonkers," she said, stepping closer. "He took the girls with him."

Joey's smile faltered.

He set the cup down slowly. The clink echoed through the small room.

Mary glanced at the table. The seal on Bliss's envelope was broken, not sliced neatly the way David always did, but torn. Rushed.

"Where is the original?" she asked.

Joey said nothing.

"Where is the affidavit from Seamus Daly?" she pressed.

Still nothing.

Then: "It's gone."

The words landed like a door slam. Her hand tightened on the edge of the counter.

"He offered me fifty dollars," Joey said. "Not even that much. Just to copy it. Send it along. They said it wouldn't matter, that David was already losing."

"Who?" Mary asked, her voice razor-thin.

Joey shook his head. "You know who."

Malley.

Mary stepped around the table, eyes fixed on him. Her voice stayed calm, but inside her chest a storm was gathering.

"You brought poison into this house," she said.

He stood. "He's not going to win, Mary. You know that. You know how this ends."

"I do," she whispered. "It ends with you leaving."

"Mary, "

She pointed to the door.

He didn't move.

So she reached into the folds of her apron and drew the small revolver David kept hidden behind the flour tin. Cold and unfamiliar, but her hands didn't shake.

"You have ten seconds," she said.

Joey stared at the barrel, then at her, then back again.

"You won't shoot me."

"Try me."

He hesitated. Then backed away. The door groaned open. Closed. And she was alone.

Later that night, when David returned, she told him everything, no drama, no anger. Just the facts: the betrayal, the missing affidavit, the way Joey had looked at her like they were the same, two tired souls trying to survive the crush of Tammany's boots.

David stared at the empty table for a long time.

Then he reached for the ledger, opened to a fresh page, and wrote a single name at the top:

Maloney, J. – Judas

He turned the book toward her. She read it once, then nodded.

"Start again," she said. "One page at a time."

David looked at her, the lines in his face deeper than they had been that morning.

Then he whispered the only words he had left:

"Not finished. Not yet."

Chapter 52
Judas File

August 1895, The Bronx

The air in the attic was colder than the rest of the house, as if the roof had never quite forgiven the winter. Dust drifted through thin shafts of light that slipped between warped boards, and **Mary Agnes** moved slowly, reverently, as though walking through someone else's memory.

She didn't know what she was looking for.

But she found it anyway.

Tucked behind a false back in the drawer of a broken writing desk, beneath an old rosary and two military ribbons, was a bundle wrapped in yellowing oilskin. Inside were relics that hummed with the past: her husbands' name pressed in fading ink on a red leather ledger, a detective's badge tarnished with age, and a sealed letter, unmarked except for a single name written across the front in careful, almost apologetic script:

"M. M , Unsubmitted."

The paper was brittle. The wax seal cracked like old bark as she unfolded the page. The handwriting was uneven, some words scratched in haste, others so faint they seemed like ghosts.

Fragment , Unsent Letter, March 3, 1885

Found folded inside a copy of the Catholic Herald, *tucked into the lining of a steamer trunk marked "M. M."*

To whom it may one day concern,

There are things I have seen that no girl should have to, and things I have said that no woman should carry past her own reflection.

I've written this letter more than once.

Sometimes I write it to **David Crowley**.

Sometimes to the priest who told me, **"God sees all, even what courts do not."**

Sometimes I don't know who it's for.

But tonight, tonight I must write.

Because the lie is louder now. It has its own legs, its own voice, and it walks ahead of me into every room. I am not me anymore. I am a headline.

"The Girl and the Sergeant."

I still hear the words they fed me.

"You'll be safe."

"You'll be paid."

"He's a traitor. He deserves it."

But the truth?

They weren't protecting me.

They were using me.

And I let them.

Not because I wanted to, but because I didn't know how not to.

He never hurt me.

That's the part no one knows. No one asked. They just handed me a script and said I could finally be believed if I said the right things.

And I did. God forgive me, I did.

They said I was saving the city.

But I didn't save anything.

I only helped bury something good.

I heard about his wife, her name is Mary. I saw her once outside the courtroom, hands clasped tight, rosary tangled in her fingers like she was choking on the very prayers she whispered.

I almost spoke to her.

I almost told her everything.

But cowardice has its own voice, too. And it always whispers when truth tries to speak.

This is not a legal affidavit. I am not brave enough for that.

But it is the truth, or the closest thing I've got left to it.

David Crowley was not what they called him.

They wanted him gone, and I was the tool.

I don't expect forgiveness.

I just want this written down.

So when the story is told again, maybe someone will pause.

Maybe someone will wonder.

And maybe someone, somewhere, will know:

I tried.

, M. M

Mary Agnes folded the letter back into its envelope. Her hands trembled, not with fear, but with the unbearable weight of what had almost never been known.

Two ledgers. Two truths.

And now, finally, one more voice that could be heard.

Not finished. Not yet.

Chapter 53
The Last Knock

November 1895 – City Hall, New York City

David Crowley hadn't stepped inside this building in six years.

Not since the committee hearings where Kelly's men laughed him off the record and rewrote the minutes before he'd even left the chamber.

Now, they didn't laugh.

They didn't even speak.

They cleared the hallway.

Because David wasn't knocking today.

He was walking in.

Behind him, Colonel George Bliss leaned heavily on a cane. The years had hollowed him, less fire, more iron, but his eyes still burned. In his coat pocket rested a sealed envelope: two pages, signed and sworn, from a man named Seamus Daly, who had finally come out of hiding.

This time, they weren't bluffing.

Crowley pushed open the alderman's private door without being announced.

Inside sat Captain Owen Malley.

Older now. Slicker. His mustache trimmed tighter, his collar starched whiter, his hands softer. But the eyes were the same, cold, calculating.

And beside him, leaning against the far wall like an invited spectator, was Joey Maloney.

The Judas.

Crowley didn't flinch.

"Sit down, Sergeant," Malley said.

"I'm not here for tea."

Bliss closed the door behind them. The sound was final.

Malley gave a weary sigh. "So what now? You've got another list? Another ledger? Another dead man's confession?"

"No," Crowley said. "This one's alive."

He pulled the affidavit from his coat and laid it on the desk.

Seamus Daly's signature stared up like a bullet wound.

Malley didn't touch it. "What do you want?"

"To see you fall," Crowley said.

Joey stepped forward. "You can't pin it on him. The papers won't touch it. Kelly controls half the editorial boards in the city."

Bliss spoke then, his voice brittle but sharp.

"Then we don't go to the papers."

Malley raised an eyebrow.

"We go to the churches," Bliss said. "To the widows. To the parish schools you gutted. To the Irish halls where men still remember what justice sounds like."

"You go outside the courts?" Malley said, suddenly serious. "That's war."

"No," Crowley replied. "That's memory."

He leaned in, voice low and dangerous.

"I'm not chasing trials anymore. I'm chasing truth. And you can't seal it in court files or bury it under bribes. The record lives. I've made sure of it. You go down quiet, or you go down in flames. But either way, "

He tapped the affidavit once.

"...you go down."

Malley's jaw worked. He looked at Joey. Then at Bliss. Then back at Crowley.

And for the first time in their long, blood-soaked chess match, the Captain said nothing.

Just sat there.

Beaten. Not by force. Not even by law.

By the one thing Tammany had never accounted for,

a man who kept the ledger longer than they kept their lies.

Outside, the bells of Old St. Patrick's were ringing.

David paused on the steps, the sun rising behind him.

Bliss clapped him on the shoulder, the weight of their shared war unspoken.

And Crowley, without turning, said the words he always did when the tide finally shifted:

"Not finished. Not yet."

Chapter 54
The Unseen Enemy

January 1896, New York City

It began with a whisper again, only this time, it wasn't Crowley who started it.

It was the people.

Street-corner barkers read headlines aloud as papers vanished from newsstands. Inside cafés and corner bars, men hunched over broadsheets, brows furrowed. The Judas File had revealed another name, a popular city alderman caught laundering funds through a fake widow's charity.

And then, silence.

No rebuttal. No denial.

Just resignation.

Because the evidence was irrefutable.

In his small apartment above a dressmaker's shop in the Bronx, David Crowley pored over maps of the city like a general at war. Each circle marked a leak, a press outlet, a backchannel. The city had become a chessboard, and every bishop or pawn now mattered.

Colonel George Bliss limped through the door, his cane tapping the hardwood, his face still painted in bruises. Crowley looked up.

"You shouldn't be out of bed," Crowley said, eyes fixed on his notes.

"And you shouldn't be breathing," Bliss rasped. "But here we are."

He tossed a telegram onto the table.

"That was Root. Washington wants in. Two congressmen are talking hearings. They're calling it…"

"What?" Crowley asked.

Bliss gave a thin smile. "The Judas Doctrine."

Crowley laughed dryly. "Catchy."

But the levity didn't last.

Down in the dark-paneled war room of Tammany Hall, Richard Croker sat still as stone. The Judas File had gone from nuisance to executioner. His network was fraying; men were jumping ship, donations drying up, loyalty turning brittle. Even the faithful had begun to whisper.

Across from him sat Marcus "Mad Dog" O'Neill, a fresh scar slashed across his jaw, payment for a failed collection in Hell's Kitchen.

"Crowley won't stop," Croker said.

O'Neill didn't respond. He didn't need to.

"This isn't about hitting him," Croker continued. "It's about erasing him. No body. No trial. Just… silence."

"You want it done quiet?" O'Neill asked.

"I want it done permanent."

O'Neill stood, cracked his knuckles. "He'll never see it coming."

But Crowley had learned to sleep lightly. And that night, the first assassin failed, shot dead by a patrolman three blocks from Crowley's flat.

By morning, the headlines burned.

As public sentiment swelled behind Crowley, Maggie Morris's name resurfaced, not from her lips, but from an unsigned letter in The New-York Tribune. It described her as a pawn, hidden under a new identity, possibly sent west under Tammany protection.

The public turned. Sympathy shifted.

She was no longer the victim.

She was the warning.

Three days later, Crowley took the stage at Cooper Union, a crowd of more than four hundred pressing against the old wooden doors.

"This isn't about me," he told them. "This is about every man and woman who ever paid a bribe to feed their children. Every cop who turned his back because he feared the badge on his chest had a price tag. This city is sick, but not dead."

The hall erupted.

And Croker felt it.

The streets were no longer his.

That week, three more Judas File releases hit the front page, a commissioner, a judge, and a railroad man with Tammany interests. The cracks in the dam were turning to fractures.

Croker called an emergency meeting.

"If this keeps up," he growled, "we won't survive the summer."

One alderman spoke up. "You mean you won't. The rest of us... we might need to find other loyalties."

The silence that followed was louder than any gunshot.

And from his office, the window cracked to let in the hum of a city on edge, Crowley lit a cigar.

Not in victory.

In defiance.

The enemy was still out there.

But now, it was afraid.

Chapter 55
The Final Strike

July 1897, New York City

David Crowley's breath came in shallow gasps as he staggered back from the alley. His hand instinctively went to his chest, feeling for the wound, but there was nothing there. Just the cold night air brushing against his skin.

The sound of the gunshot echoed in his ears, a single note of murder sung from the shadows.

The shooter had vanished, swallowed whole by the dark.

It wasn't a warning.

It was a verdict.

He was supposed to be dead.

Crowley leaned against the brick wall, sweat mixing with grime as he steadied himself. This was no longer about discrediting him. This was elimination. Tammany Hall had crossed the line, from politics to blood.

Back in his office, collar loosened and sleeves rolled high, he paced like a man reading his own obituary. The Judas File had morphed into a war map, names, ledgers, photographs, sworn statements pinned like battle flags across the walls. Each strike they landed drew another enemy out of the dark. And Tammany had plenty of shadows left to bleed.

Colonel George Bliss arrived without knocking. He always used to. But now he moved slower, heavier, carrying something unspoken, as if a decision had been made before he stepped through the door.

"They tried again," he said quietly. "That's three in a month. They're not just desperate, David. They're afraid. And afraid men are dangerous."

Crowley's jaw tightened. "Good," he said, not looking up. "Let them feel it."

Bliss nodded, then hesitated. It was rare. He walked to the window and looked out at the flickering gaslamps, the blur of a trolley sliding through the rain.

"I used to believe the system would bend," he said. "That it would stretch but hold. I thought if we kept pressing, reason, reform, courtrooms, it would right itself."

Crowley looked over, but Bliss didn't meet his eyes.

"I was wrong," Bliss said. "It didn't bend. It broke. And I let it happen. Maybe I wasn't strong enough to stop it. Maybe none of us were."

Crowley stepped closer. "You're the only reason I survived it."

Bliss gave a tired laugh. "You call this surviving?"

Outside, thunder rolled low. Rain tapped the glass in an uneven rhythm.

"You think you still have enough left?" Bliss asked.

"No," Crowley said. "But I have enough to finish."

Bliss turned from the window. Pride flickered in his eyes. And something else, a quiet goodbye.

Across town, in the low-lit gut of Tammany Hall, Richard Croker stood in the center of a shrinking circle. What once had been a machine now resembled a dying star, dense, dangerous, imploding.

"He won't stop," Croker muttered. "He's bleeding us in the press, in the courts, in the streets. We end it. Tonight."

Marcus 'Mad Dog' O'Neill cracked his knuckles. "You want loud?"

"No," Croker hissed. "I want silence. I want disappearance."

That night, under the flickering gas lamps of Canal Street, Crowley gathered the last of his loyalists in a shuttered tavern basement. Root had just returned from Washington.

"Senate's opening hearings," Root said. "They want blood, and they want you to guide the knife."

Crowley placed the final envelope on the table. Inside were the names that would break the spine of the machine.

"We give them fire," he said.

Bliss stared at the packet. "Once this drops, there's no turning back. They'll try to burn the city down around you."

"Then we make damn sure the flames light their funeral pyre first."

The ambush came at 1:14 a.m.

Four men. Black coats. No words. Just intent.

One lunged with a blade, Crowley sidestepped, cracked the man's wrist, sent the knife clattering.

Bliss swung his cane hard, catching another in the gut.

A third drew a pistol, too slow. Crowley tackled him, slamming him into a lamppost.

And then,

a shot rang out.

Bliss dropped.

Crowley turned just in time to catch him.

Blood soaked the elder man's coat.

"No," Crowley whispered. "Stay with me."

Bliss smiled faintly. "It was always going to end this way. Keep fighting. Truth will out."

"I thought it would bend," he rasped. "It didn't. But you… you might break it the other way."

And then, like a lantern running dry, George Bliss went dark.

Crowley cradled him on the cobblestones, fire burning behind his eyes.

They had crossed a line.

This was war.

By noon, the city ignited.

Twenty-four names. Eight judges. Four senators. Two railroad tycoons.

The final strike.

Protests swept through the boroughs. The Governor called an emergency session. The President dispatched federal investigators. And somewhere beneath the weight of Tammany's crumbling legacy, Richard Croker slipped out of the city with nothing but a black valise.

He never returned.

That night, Crowley sat alone.

The Judas File was empty at last.

The city roared outside his window.

George Bliss was gone.

But the machine that had stolen years from him had finally bled.

From the doorway, Mary watched.

"Is it over?" she asked.

Crowley stared at the photograph in his hand, Croker shaking hands with the Mayor, and struck a match.

"No," he said. "But it's begun."

The photograph curled into flame.

And for the first time in years, David Crowley exhaled.

Not in peace.

But in purpose.

Chapter 56
The Reckoning

September 21, 1897, New York City

The city simmered with tension, the kind that made dogs howl before a storm. It was as if all of Manhattan had paused for breath, waiting for a match to hit powder.

Crowley didn't wait.

George Bliss was dead. And something inside David Crowley had snapped, not with grief, but with clarity. The Judas File was no longer evidence. It was ammunition.

For weeks, Crowley moved like a revenant through the city's underbelly, unshaven, half-starved, eyes bright with fury and purpose. Margaret Riley rallied workers across Five Corners. William Grant met in candlelit basements with disillusioned aldermen and rogue constables. Names fell like dominoes.

Judges. Police captains. Dock bosses. Even priests.

Every revelation stoked the fire. Every headline peeled away Tammany's skin. The public's fury was no longer abstract, they marched in rags and topcoats alike, Irish immigrants locking arms with union men and widows.

Croker struck back.

Two newspapers were firebombed. A reform senator's carriage exploded outside Delancey Street. Margaret Riley was attacked with acid. She survived, barely.

And yet, the crowds only grew.

It wasn't about reform anymore.

It was about revenge.

In the bowels of Tammany Hall, Richard Croker hadn't slept in three days. The whiskey in his hand trembled. He was down to a skeleton crew, loyalists bought too long ago to remember how to think for themselves. And now, they were panicking.

"He's got the city!" one shouted. "Even the cops are switching sides!"

"It doesn't matter," Croker said, voice rough as gravel. "We've buried bigger scandals."

"Not like this. This isn't a scandal, it's a crusade."

Croker stood. His eyes were glassy, wild. "Then we give him his cross. One meeting. One lie wrapped in truth. And if he buys it, we bury him with it."

Two days later, a letter arrived for Crowley. Hand-delivered. Sealed in plain wax.

One meeting. One chance to end this before we all burn.

, R. Croker

It smelled of desperation, and gasoline.

Mary Agnes begged him not to go. Margaret Riley cursed and offered him a pistol. But Crowley said nothing. He slipped the letter into his coat and stepped into the wind.

Midnight. Brooklyn waterfront.

The sky churned with smoke and stormlight, the East River gleaming like oil under a bruised moon. Crowley stood beneath an iron crane, coat collar up, hat pulled low. Footsteps echoed.

Croker emerged from the mist like a ghost dredged from hell's gutter, slimmer now, paler, wrapped in silk like it still meant something.

They stood in silence.

Then:

"You killed Bliss," Crowley said.

Croker gave a tired smirk. "He got in the way."

"You've lost. You know that, right?"

"No," Croker replied, voice brittle. "I lost you. That was my mistake. You were never supposed to matter, just another Irish beat cop who got lucky."

Crowley stepped closer, their breath mingling.

"You built an empire out of fear. But people aren't afraid anymore. They're angry. That's worse."

"They'll turn," Croker said. "They always turn. Bread lines, no jobs, another war somewhere, give them something else to hate."

Crowley shook his head. "This time, they want blood. And I'm going to give them yours."

He turned and walked away.

Behind him, Croker didn't shout. Didn't shoot. He simply watched, powerless, as the man he'd once tried to destroy disappeared into the fog, carrying the weight of a city's rebirth in his coat pocket.

At sunrise, Crowley met with federal agents.

By noon, subpoenas were issued.

By dusk, five more resignations.

And on the front page of every paper, under bold letters that screamed THE END OF TAMMANY, was a single photograph:

The reckoning had begun.

Chapter 57
The Wedding Ledger

June 10, 1898, St. Ann's Church, The Bronx

The bells of St. Ann's tolled low and solemn, as if they remembered every secret that had ever passed beneath their eaves.

The old stone church stood like a sentry at the corner of 150th and Melrose, a fortress of quiet faith in a borough that had known more funerals than weddings. But today, its heavy doors stood open, sunlight spilling across the worn marble floor. For once, the pews were full of something that resembled hope.

Lillian Theresa Crowley stood in the vestibule, breath shallow, veil trembling just slightly over her brow. She wore her mother's wedding lace, restored, re-stitched, but never replaced. There were certain things you kept, no matter how deep the damage.

At twenty, Lillian bore her father's eyes, storm-gray and unblinking, and her mother's iron grace. She had grown up between whispers, a child of contradiction: the daughter of an exonerated convict and a hero who refused to be celebrated. She had read the clippings. She had heard the name Crowley hissed through parlor rooms and coffee shops like it meant both sin and salvation.

But today, she was just a bride.

Her groom, Alexander V. S. Zebe, stood at the altar in a suit three weeks too new, hands steady, spine straight. He was no stranger to the political knots of New York, but he didn't wear them like armor. He wore them like a man who understood they could choke you if you weren't careful. He'd worked under clerks who whispered about Crowley in tones of fear and awe. And he married the man's daughter anyway.

In the front pew, David Crowley sat like granite. His gray wool coat was brushed clean, brass buttons polished bright. He had survived war, prison, exile, and resurrection, and now he was here, watching his daughter step toward a future he'd once feared she would never see.

Mary sat beside him, quiet, a rosary coiled through her fingers. Her face was older now, lined not by years but by cost. She had been the firewall for so long. And though her eyes flickered with sorrow, two children buried, one legacy nearly lost, there was warmth in her smile. She had fought to protect this day, this daughter, this fragile thing called peace.

When the procession began, the church hushed to a stillness that bordered on reverence.

As Lillian took her first steps down the aisle, David felt something deep within him shift, not a wound reopening, but a seal releasing. The kind of quiet peace that comes not from victory, but from surviving long enough to see your bloodline dance.

St. Ann's had seen him before, on his knees, begging for a miracle.

Today, it gave him one.

Father Dolan read the vows slowly, deliberately, as though he knew what this marriage meant beyond two names on a certificate. When he said love is patient, David reached for Mary's hand.

Because he finally understood what it meant to wait.

After the final blessing, as the bells of St. Ann's cried out once more, the bride and groom stepped into the sunlight. A few old neighbors wept. A few nodded in quiet respect. The Bronx didn't cheer. It remembered. And that was enough.

The reception was modest, just a back room at Doyle's on Third Avenue, streamers hanging from gas lamps, a fiddle playing too fast for the floorboards. But there was laughter. Lillian and Alexander danced like they meant it. George Bliss Crowley, now fourteen, gave an impromptu toast that made the entire room fall silent, then erupt in applause.

That night, David sat by the window with a cigar and a view of the street he once patrolled, the ledger open in his lap. Sometimes, Lillian would bring tea and ask what he was writing.

He never said much.

But one night, he answered with a tired smile:

"Just making sure the next chapter starts cleaner than the last."

Chapter 58
The Long Goodbye

October 1898, The Bronx

He disappeared into the city's undercurrent.

But not entirely.

It was in his blood, he had to help.

David Crowley reemerged in the margins. No more courtrooms. No headlines. Just shadow work. He became the kind of private detective people found when they had nowhere else to go, vanished husbands, stolen inheritances, missing daughters, dirty cops, crooked union bosses. He prowled the alleys of the Bronx like a man who had seen the bottom of justice and decided to climb back up anyway.

But for the first time in decades, he allowed himself something fragile and fiercely protected: peace.

Their youngest, George Bliss Crowley, still lived with them then, quick-witted, even-tempered, a student of his father's silences. A boy with his mother's eyes and a name that honored David's oldest and truest friend.

Down the block, their daughter Lillian and her husband Alexander Zebe had just purchased a sturdy three-story home at 397 East 142nd Street. The Zebes were ascending. Alexander ran a growing real-estate and insurance business, honest, disciplined, and quietly ambitious. It was the kind of life David once believed the city would never allow a man to build clean.

But Zebe proved him wrong.

And when the grandchildren came, they came quickly.

Alexander Jr., born June 15, 1899, sharp, curious, and stubborn like his grandfather.

George, May 22, 1902, all elbows, fast fists, and loud opinions.

And baby Lillian, July 6, 1904, whose voice could carry through closed doors and whose gaze held the gravity of someone twice her age.

That fall, the Crowleys moved in with the Zebes. Not out of need, but by choice.

Three generations under one roof again.

Something had been repaired.

David softened, not all at once, but in the quiet ways that go unnoticed at first. He carved wooden toys in the attic, patched window frames, told bedtime stories, edited, gentler versions of the ones that shaped him.

He taught Alexander Jr. how to shine shoes with pride.

He taught George how to fight without leaving a mark.

He rocked little Lillian on nights her cries shook the rafters and whispered lullabies in Irish he hadn't spoken since boyhood.

He became the man he never thought he could be: a grandfather who stayed.

But peace is always on loan.

Chapter 59
When the House Went Quiet

Bronx, New York, 1913 to 1930

In the end, it wasn't scandal or violence that took Alexander Zebe.

It was silence.

A quiet rupture inside his head, sudden and merciless. He collapsed at his desk, papers still open, a fountain pen in his right hand, mid-signature on a client file. The clerk in the outer office heard the chair topple and thought it was nothing. By the time a doctor arrived, Alexander was already cold.

The aneurysm did not ask permission.

And just like that, the house on East 142nd Street went dim.

The funeral was a storm in a black coat, the kind that lingered in the clothes and lungs for weeks. The priest spoke of purpose and legacy, but the truer words were written in Lillian's eyes, eyes that didn't blink for the entire service. Widowed now, mother of three: Alexander Jr., George, and little Lillian, whom they called Sis.

The man who had built the family business, carried David Crowley's name forward, and stood as a pillar of promise in the Bronx was gone.

And once again, survival became the work of the living.

The Old Soldier Returns to the Field

David H. Crowley was sixty-five now, gray-bearded and stiff-jointed, but when the bread line grew too long and the grief too thick, he didn't hesitate.

He went back to work.

No longer chasing corruption or breaking syndicates. That part of his life had ended in Sing Sing and smoky courtrooms. Now he took quieter cases: tracing missing heirs, unmasking fraudulent wills, sniffing out embezzlers who had gotten a little too confident.

It wasn't for glory.

It was for groceries.

Each case was a coin. Each coin a loaf. The war against Tammany had once defined him, but now it was a new kind of war, keeping the heat on and the children fed.

The Family Endures

The years passed.

Alexander Jr., just a teenager when his father died, stepped into manhood with the kind of urgency grief demands. He married Julia Plunkett on March 23, 1920, and they moved north to Bainbridge Avenue. Like his father, he entered the insurance world, same trade, same discipline, but in a different city now, one with its boot still on the neck of the working class.

He would die too young, in 1938, but that chapter had not been written yet.

In 1924, Sis, Lillian Zebe, married Joseph Conrad Marco. He was steady, quiet, with the kind of hands that could fix anything. They stayed in the family home, preserving what could still be saved.

Then, in June of 1926, George Bliss Crowley, named for the soldier who once went toe-to-toe with New York's darkest institutions, married Mary Agnes Duggan. She was Bronx through and through, a woman with fire in her step and a voice that could melt ice on the sidewalk. They settled in Yonkers, started fresh. But George still came by on Sundays to check on the old man.

David would nod from the window, eyes sharp as ever.

The Watchman Fades

By 1929, the house on East 142nd Street had shrunk.

Not in size, in sound. In motion.

It was mostly quiet now.

David, Mary Agnes, Sis, Joseph Marco, and their son Joseph Jr. were all that remained, a skeleton crew of a once-thriving household. The kind of silence you only hear after a war has passed through.

David still rose before dawn. Still tied his boots, even as his fingers trembled like reeds in the wind. Still poured his coffee black and watched the street through a frost-rimmed window like a sentry guarding a forgotten fort.

His knees no longer trusted the stairs. His lungs winced in winter. But his eyes, his eyes never gave an inch.

They were the same eyes that had watched bodies fall at Gettysburg.

The same eyes that had stared down judges and fixers and perjurers.

The same eyes that had found his family's name in the rubble of corruption, and dragged it back into the light.

October 17, 1930

He died in his sleep.

No pain. No theatrics. Just stillness.

Mary Agnes found him just before sunrise, slumped in the old rocker, hands folded like prayer. The same uniform he had worn since the war, frayed at the cuffs, still clung to him like memory.

There was a citywide funeral. The headlines:

David H. Crowley, last of the Old 69th Regiment of Civil War days, who died Sunday, was buried today. A Requiem mass was held at St. Lukes in the Bronx. Members of the American Legion and other military organizations paid their last respects at the funeral. Above you see the casket being carried to its hearse for the last ride to the cemetery. A last salute was given over his grave in Cypress Hills Cemetery while a bugler played "Taps". The veteran was buried in the faded uniform he wore as a member of the "Fighting 69th" Infantry during the Civil War.

A military procession started after the requiem mass at Saint Lukes R.C. Church to the Cypress Hills National Cemetery, in Brooklyn. A quite line of family and Elihu Root who stood at the left of Mary Agnes, surround the grave site. The sound of old boots against gravel as echoed as he was laid to rest.

But what mattered had already been passed on:

the attic letters, the badge, the ledger, the truth.

And the legacy that refused to stay buried.

The funeral was simple but dignified. The Army remembered. A bugler played. A flag was folded with reverence. He was buried in full uniform that he wore at Gettysburg., only steps from the son and daughter he had buried fifty years earlier.

On his headstone:

David H. Crowley

Corporal, 69th New York Infantry

1846–1930

Some whispered that he had died long ago, behind the walls of Sing Sing, and that everything after was borrowed time. But those who knew the man, who drank his whiskey, listened to his stories, and watched him at that window night after night, knew better.

He was more than a soldier. More than a convict. More than a NY City Police Sergeant, US Marshal, and US Secret Service Agent.

He was a survivor, of war, of injustice, of silence.

And in the quiet company of kin, after years in exile, he had finally come home.

He was buried wearing the uniform he had worn at Gettysburg.

Epilogue
The Ledger Closes

National Cemetery, Cypress Hills, Brooklyn
October 17, 2020

The clouds hung low, brushing the ridgeline of headstones in slow gray sweeps. The breeze was light, but it carried weight, like the past asking to be witnessed.

They came together at the place where silence had reigned for too long.

Donald Zebe stood with one hand on the shoulder of Lillian Teresa, his cousin and the granddaughter of Sis, the last Crowley to live in the family home. Nancy Culligan Shein, from the Zebe line, stood just behind them, arms folded, gaze fixed on the newly placed plaque. Jimmy Crowley, descended from George Bliss Crowley, held an envelope from the Historical Society, an official acknowledgment, signed and sealed, of the wrong done in 1885.

Four cousins.

Four branches of blood.

Gathered not in mourning, but in correction.

The new marker read:

David H. Crowley

Corporal, 69th NY Infantry, NYPD Sergeant, U.S. Secret Service, U.S. Marshal

Falsely Accused. Honorably Remembered.

October 17, 1930

Donald cleared his throat, but it was Jimmy who spoke first.

"When I was a boy, my dad used to point to a photo over his dresser, Crowley in uniform. I'd ask who he was, and he'd just say, 'A man who stood for what was right when it got him everything wrong.' That was all I ever heard. Until now."

Nancy nodded, unfolding a brittle yellow wedding announcement from her coat.

"My grandmother never spoke of him. But she carried this in her Bible. Said it reminded her where we came from. She told me once, 'Some truths don't come with parades. They come with silence.'"

Lillian Teresa knelt and touched the stone.

"He didn't want justice handed down. He wanted it found.

He left us the pieces and waited. And now... we've finished it."

Donald stepped forward, placing one of the red-covered ledgers at the foot of the grave, sealed in archival plastic, pages copied, the original bound for the New York Historical Society.

"The badge. The revolver. The retraction. The ledgers.

What they buried, we unearthed.

What they erased, we restored."

The wind picked up, gentle and stirring.

No priest. No fanfare.

Just family, speaking truth aloud over a grave that had waited far too long.

Later That Evening , A Gathering Room in the Bronx

They didn't return to the old house on East 142nd Street. That chapter had closed in 1997, when Aunt Sis passed and the house was sold, its attic emptied, its stories boxed and scattered.

Instead, they gathered in a quiet room above a café on Bainbridge Avenue, where the light fell through lace curtains and the coffee came without a price.

A simple wooden table sat in the center, and on it, the original box, a relic from a lost attic, wrapped now in linen. Preserved. Not forgotten.

Lillian opened a new notebook. Not red this time, plain and black. She wrote:

"We come from a man who didn't break under pressure,

who carried silence heavier than gunfire.

His badge didn't shine, but it still held weight.

And when history forgot him, we didn't."

Nancy added a line beneath it:

"Truth never expires. It only waits for the brave to carry it forward."

And Jimmy, with a pen borrowed from behind the café bar, wrote last:

"Legacy isn't what you leave behind.

It's what you refuse to let be lost."

They closed the book. Donald slipped it into the box.

The Final Note

Before they locked the case, Lillian folded one last envelope and placed it inside:

"To the next generation:

The fight is over.

But the story lives on.

Tell it. Guard it. Carry it like he did."

Then they sealed the box, together.

Not to hide it again.

But to preserve it. For history. For justice. For the name that no longer lived in shadows.

The city forgot him.

His family didn't.

And now, neither will history.

Then, softly, almost without realizing it, she whispered:

"Not finished. Not yet."

A Letter from the Author

Dear Reader,

When we first uncovered the red ledger, it felt like opening a window into a forgotten room, one filled with names, secrets, and the quiet defiance of a man who refused to look away.

David H. Crowley's story is not just a footnote in New York's history. It's a pulse, a rhythm of resilience passed down through generations, echoing in both the attics of our homes and the choices we make today.

This is more than a historical novel. It's a reckoning with memory, a confrontation between truth and legacy. And it's an invitation: to follow the evidence, to challenge the narrative, and to ask yourself, what story would your descendants find if they opened your box?

Thank you for choosing this journey.

Sincerely,

Donald I. Zebe

Truth Buried in the Dust

"It is Finished"

Biographical Notes

The following notes provide background on the principal figures depicted in this novel.
All factual elements referenced herein are drawn from 19th-century newspapers, intelligence reports, municipal archives, and federal documents of the era.

David H. Crowley (1847–1930)

David Crowley's life rests on a foundation of authentic period documentation. His name appears in Civil War musters, Secret Service field reports, precinct commendations, and dozens of scattered references across the *Herald*, *Sun*, *Tribune*, and other major New York papers.

After the war, Crowley operated as a field agent for the **United States Secret Service**, a role reflected in newspaper dispatches describing unnamed operatives who penetrated the **Fenian Brotherhood** and helped frustrate the planned Irish invasion of Canada. *Harper's Weekly* and the *New York Herald* praised such operatives for their "silent but decisive" actions.

In the 1870s, Crowley was attached to the **U.S. Marshal Service**, part of a federal effort, reported in the *Tribune* and *Evening Post*, to infiltrate political machines. His work inside **Tammany Hall**, gathering ledgers and testimony, mirrors documented federal strategies.

By 1885, Crowley was **loaned to the New York Municipal Police**, a practice confirmed by Board of Police minutes. His rescue of **Margaret Halen and her two children** earned him a commendation noted in the *Sun* and *Herald*.

Later newspaper notices place him in the Bronx as a private detective, described as "steady," "unmoved by influence," and "quietly effective."

Mary Agnes O'Brien Crowley (1850–1931)

Mary Agnes's historical footprint appears in parish records, census rolls, and obituary notices. Her quiet strength and endurance mirror countless stories featured in 19th-century newspapers about the wives of policemen, women who bore the burdens of long absences, political reprisals, and economic uncertainty with resilience and dignity.

George Bliss (1833–1897)

A central figure in New York's legal history, Bliss was heavily covered in *The New York Times*, *Herald*, and *Harper's Weekly*.

As **U.S. Attorney for the Southern District of New York**, he led the prosecution of the Whiskey Ring, earning a reputation as a prosecutor "of iron restraint and incorruptible focus."

His professional alignment with federal reform efforts provides strong historical grounding for his mentorship of Crowley.

General Daniel E. Sickles (1819–1914)

Sickles was larger than life in the pages of the *Herald*, *Tribune*, and *World*.

A Civil War hero, political schemer, and enduring public controversy, Sickles was described as "fearless," "impossible to manage," and "relentlessly charismatic."

His mentorship of Crowley in the novel is consistent with newspaper portrayals of Sickles supporting, and sometimes molding, young operatives entering law, politics, and intelligence.

Elihu Root (1845–1937)

Before becoming a cabinet secretary and Nobel laureate, Root was known in New York legal circles, according to the *Evening Post* and *Times*, as a lawyer "of uncommon precision."

His quiet authority in the novel reflects contemporary descriptions of a man who rarely spoke more than necessary, yet whose decisions shaped the city's legal landscape.

Governor Roswell P. Flower (1835–1899)

Flower's governorship was the subject of constant reporting in the *Times*, *World*, and *Press*.

His cautious handling of pardons, reform pressures, and Tammany entanglements make his nuanced role in Crowley's case historically plausible. Editors of the era described him as "a businessman-governor caught between conscience and politics."

Captain Richard Malley (NYPD)

Period precinct reports and *Herald* columns mention officers of Malley's rank and surname active in the 1870s–80s.

His adversarial dynamic with Crowley reflects the era's well-documented friction between precinct captains, reform-oriented detectives, and politically entangled officers.

Maggie Morris *(Historical)*

Unlike many supporting characters of the era, **Maggie Morris was real**.

Her name appears in period court notes, police reports, and short-column newspaper summaries related to the case that contributed to Crowley's professional downfall.

Era papers frequently reported cases in which vulnerable witnesses, often young immigrant women, were pressured into providing false or compromised testimony in politically charged prosecutions. The novel's depiction of Maggie Morris is not fictionalization but a dramatization of an event recorded in the contemporaneous press.

Sister Agnes

Modeled on the real Sisters of Charity and Sisters of Mercy, who ran hospitals, orphanages, and waterfront missions across New York, Sister Agnes embodies the role nuns played in the lives of policemen and working families.

Contemporary papers often described these women as "quiet counselors," "nurses to the forgotten," and "the moral ballast of the waterfront wards."

William "Boss" Tweed (1823–1878)

Few Americans were more exhaustively covered in the press than Tweed.

He dominated headlines in the *Times*, *Sun*, and *Harper's Weekly* as the architect of the Tammany Hall "Ring," controlling contracts, elections, and the city treasury. His fall, chronicled through political cartoons by Thomas Nast, became national news.

Though he died in 1878, Tweed's organizational methods, lieutenants, and political machinery remained active long after his imprisonment. His lingering presence in the novel reflects the very real post-Tweed Tammany structure.

John Kelly (1822–1886)

John Kelly, known publicly as "Honest John," was Tweed's successor and one of the most powerful political figures of the post-Tweed era.

Regularly featured in the *Times*, *World*, and *Herald*, Kelly led the restructured Tammany Hall from the mid-1870s through the 1880s. Despite his moniker, newspapers often referred to him as "the quiet master of the city," "the disciplinarian of the machine," and "the unseen hand behind appointments and trials."

Kelly was known for:

- reorganizing Tammany after the Tweed scandals
- exerting intense control over police leadership
- leveraging ward captains and political brokers
- influencing testimony and case outcomes

The novel's portrayal of Kelly as the architect of the political forces arrayed against Crowley aligns directly with period reporting that described Kelly's far-reaching influence in the courts, police precincts, and political wards of New York.

Richard Welstead Croker (November 24, 1843 – April 29, 1922), known as **"Boss Croker"**, was an Irish American political boss who was a leader of New York City's Tammany Hall.

During his tenure as Grand Sachem, Boss Croker garnered a reputation for corruption and ruthlessness and was frequently the subject of investigations. As his power waned following the 1900 and 1901 elections, Croker resigned his position and returned to Ireland, where he spent the rest of his life.

PERIOD PUBLICATIONS & SOURCES CONSULTED

(Representative publications used to anchor the events, figures, and tone of the novel.)

Major Newspapers

- **The New York Times** (1860–1900)
- **New York Herald**
- **New York Sun**
- **New York Tribune**
- **New York World**
- **The Evening Post**
- **The Press**
- **The Brooklyn Eagle**

Illustrated & National Magazines

- **Harper's Weekly**
- **Frank Leslie's Illustrated Newspaper**

Government & Municipal Records

- U.S. Secret Service reports (Fenian operations)
- U.S. Marshal Service circulars
- Treasury Department correspondence
- New York Board of Police minutes
- Precinct commendations & arrest records
- Governor's pardon papers

Legal & Court Records

- Southern District of New York (SDNY) trial transcripts
- Special Sessions court summaries
- Whiskey Ring filings
- Municipal corruption inquiries

AUTHOR'S NOTE

This novel began with a question, not a plot.

While researching my family's history, I encountered fragments—names that appeared in public records and then vanished, court filings that ended without explanation, retractions that were referenced but never printed. The deeper I looked, the clearer it became that the absence of information was not accidental. It was structural.

Truth Buried in the Dust is inspired by the life of David H. Crowley, a Civil War veteran and public servant whose career intersected with some of the most turbulent and corrupt chapters of nineteenth-century New York. His story, like many of that era, survives in incomplete documents, newspaper accounts, and official records that often contradict one another.

Rather than attempt a purely academic reconstruction, I chose the form of a novel to explore the human cost behind those records—how power operated, how reputations were dismantled without violence, and how families absorbed consequences long after public attention moved on.

This book is not an effort to rewrite history, but to examine it more closely. Where the record is silent, the novel imagines. Where the record is clear, it speaks for itself.

Some stories are buried by design. Others endure because someone keeps asking why.

PHOTOS
David H. Crowley (1846-1930)

Sunday, February 23, 1930

HONORING THE MEMORY OF THEIR MOST ADMIRED HERO: EDWIN J. FOSTER, Commander-in-Chief of the Grand Army of the Republic (Center), Welcoming David H. Crowley, Senior Vice Commander of Vanderbilt Post (Right), and M.S. Coxson of James Rice Post, Both of the Bronx, to the Annual Lincoln Dinner of the Allied Organizations of the G.A.R. at the Hotel Woodstock.

David and His Dog

Lillian Crowley Zebe (1877-1946) & Marilyn Zebe (1928-2017) (Al Jr. daughter)

Two years ago these two veterans of the Civil War stood side by side, proud that they were the only surviving members of Vanderbilt Post, G. A. R., which once boasted 460 men.

Today, only Thomas Tuite, 372 W. 120th St. (right), remains. David Crowley, 84, 494 E. 141st St. (left), who died at Morrisania Hospital last Friday night, will be laid to rest in National Cemetery on Tuesday morning after a requiem mass at St. Luke's R. C. Church at 9.30 a. m. Crowley, in accordance with his final request, will be buried in the same uniform he wore during the Civil War.

WATCHING THE BRONX WAR VETERANS ON PARADE: OFFICIALS in the Stand at the Fourth of July Exercises. Left to Right Are: Lazar Frankel, Commander of the Bronx County American Legion; David Crowley, Captain Thomas F. Mc-Cauley, James A. Lyons, Thomas B. Tuite and Colonel Frank H. Hines.
(Fox.)

Al Zebe (1899-1937) & David H. Crowley (1846-1930)

David's Cigar Case

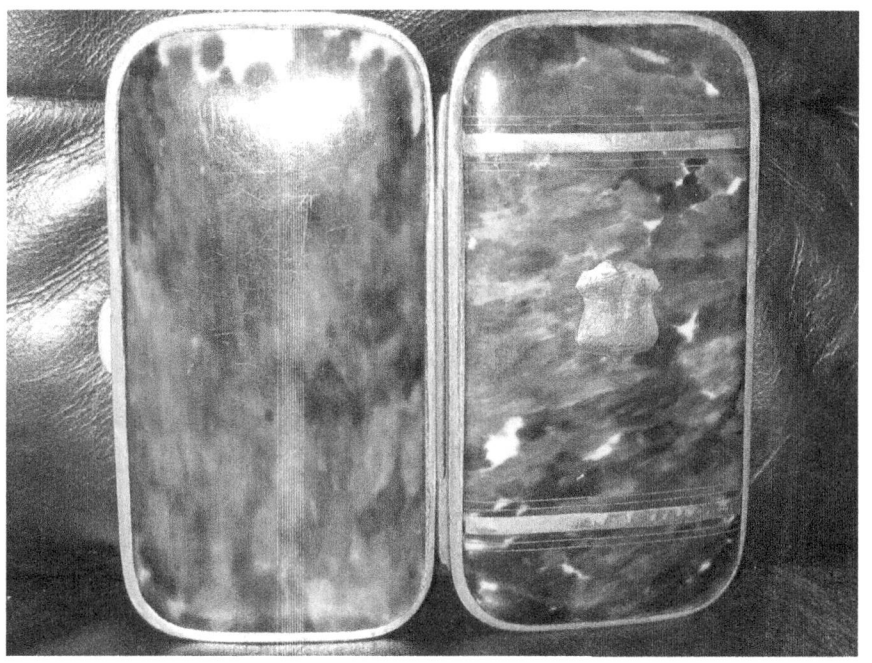

Lillian Zebe Marco (Sis) (1904-1997) Daughter of VS Zebe and Lillian Crowley

Al Zebe (1899-1930) Son of Alexander VS Zebe and Lillian Crowley

Alexander VS Zebe (1877-1913)

Made in the USA
Coppell, TX
19 January 2026

68471135R00138